Letters to Daddy

P K Bell

Letters to Daddy

Matador
5 Weir Road
Kibworth Beauchamp
Leicester LE8 0LQ, UK
Tel: 0116 279 2299
Email: books@troubador.co.uk
Web: www.troubador.co.uk/matador

ISBN 978 1906221 577

Cover design by Wendy Burton

This is a work of fiction. Any resemblance to persons either living or dead is entirely coincidental.

Typeset in 11pt Bembo by Troubador Publishing Ltd, Leicester, UK
Printed and bound in Great Britain by TJ International Ltd, Padstow, Cornwall

Matador is an imprint of Troubador Publishing Ltd

For HoneyDog, dreaming in her garden

Contents

Acknowledgements

The author would like to thank the following people for their help in producing this book:

Jeremy Thompson and the staff of Troubador
Wendy Burton for the beautiful illustrations
Paul Ferraby for the photographic enhancements
and good advice!
Lee for the additional Scottish photographs
Shirley, Jo, and Julia for the proof reading
Peter, Holly, and Delphine for listening to the story

The Beginning

Picture the scene. On an ocean far away from the grey lochs of my homeland, a mighty ship ploughs through the waves. It has been a stormy day and the sailors on board are tossed through the heaving sea on the Good Ship *Welfordia Bay*. By the evening, they are feeling tired and weary. Darkness falls and the storm blows itself out. Through the gloom, a few stars twinkle. Electro Engineer Nicholas P Kent counts them as he makes his way along the deck. Four... Five... Six. Tomorrow it will be a clear, sunny day.

He makes his way to his cabin, and throws his hard hat onto the settee. Then he pours coffee into the mug his daughter gave him for his birthday, settles down at his desk, and switches on his computer. Every evening he searches the internet for letters from his family far away at Wishing Well House in Millennium Drive. He smiles. Tonight there are three letters waiting in the mail box. There is one from Nonnie his wife, one from Grandee his father-in-law, and one from an unknown source. He frowns - he does not recognise the sender. He clicks it open and there it is... The very first of those famous...

Letters to Daddy!

Subject: A Westie Takes a Fancy to Your Sweater!

 For the attention of Electro Engineer Nicholas P Kent
@ Merchant Vessel Good Ship Welfordia Bay

Dear Daddy

Thank you so much for choosing a cute Westie such as myself to be the new family pet. I am so excited! I can't wait to meet you, so that you can admire me and marvel at my pedigree. Of course, I have a Kennel Club lineage as long as your back paw. I am the Lady Corrie-Rex Arabella Jayne o' Kerrowdown an' Drum – as per attached photograph. I think that you might have difficulty with all my names though, and humoans are noted for getting them round the wrong way. Calling me to heel on our walks in the countryside could take for ever – so I think it's best we settle for Corrie

1

just now. I know it says in 'The Puppy Dog's Handbook' that an owner should learn to respect the family dog and call it by its proper pedigree names. I think that's a tad too formal for relaxed country living these days. Don't you agree?

Masie, your dear little daughter, is excited too. You have been away all the winter and she is longing to see you again. Spring is almost here and you will be coming back. Every day she tells me that when the leaves grow on the trees, Daddy's coming home. I can hardly wait. Our family will be complete and Westies love it when that happens. We will all be together, Mummy (called Nonnie by everyone, including Masie, because she has this funny saying 'No-Ne-No-Ne-No-NO') you, dear Daddy, Grandee who lives just around the corner with his second wife Emiline, Masie, and, of course, most importantly, ME!!!

In the meantime, rest assured that I will be nice to the postman, guard your golf clubs, and continue to take a nap on your side of the huge bed upstairs. It's so big I have difficulty jumping onto it. Masie is so sweet; she lifts me up at the merest woof and snuggles me up in your nice Lucky Green Sweater. It looks so well against my gleaming white fur. I look just adorable and everyone forgets what huge dirty paws I have from rummaging in the garden beforehand. It's a dog's life!

Well, I must dash. Someone has just switched on the radio, and the kettle is boiling in the kitchen. It would not do for a puppy dawg to be caught on the internet at this time of the morning. I hope it's not doggy biscuits for tucker again today. Please let it be known that dogs **do not** eat dog food – toast and honey is just fine for a Monday morning. I shall poddle off back to my basket under the stairs and snooze through until 11am. Then Mrs P, the cleaning lady, will arrive and she always has a tit-bit in her bag for me.

Woof woofs
Corrie

| From: | EE NP Kent@MV.Welfordia Bay |
| To: | Nonnie@home.uk |

What is all this doggy nonsense? When did we get a hound? You know I hate dogs. What type is it and where did we get it from? For goodness sake get rid of it before I get home, and in the meantime get it off our bed.

Sea trip dreadful: loads of faults and bad weather, too. Thank goodness I saw this email before anyone else on board did. Humoans? Don't send me any more silly doggy stuff – it's a hard enough job as it is.

See you soon, and tell Masie I shall stop her pocket money if she wraps that dog in my best sweater again.

Nick

Reply from: Corrie Jayne@dogmail.grrr

Really, Daddy, you are bad! *Humoans* are what we dogs call you and just re-read your email and you will see what we mean! You must have jumped out of the wrong side of the dog basket this morning. I know the feeling well! Fortunately I managed to delete your letter to Nonnie before any harm was done.

Please note that I am NOT a hound. Hounds howl, sniff along imaginary trails for hours, and very probably fetch sticks that are thrown for them. Westies do not do that sort of thing. They are far too smart. Westies like comfort, regular meals, walkies, going out in the car for shopping trips and such, but above all KINDNESS AND KNOWING THEY ARE DOGGY ADORED! How are you fixed?

Woof woofs
Corrie

 Reply from: EE NP Kent@MV.Welfordia Bay

Hello Fur Face

This is outrageous!!! Nonnie, if this is not you on the internet it must be Masie. This *humoan* is now very impressed and promises not to grumble or moan about things again! Masie, when did you learn to write such good letters? I could not write such a good letter when I was eight. Well done!

So it's a game? All right, I will play along with it for now. It looks as though I have a magical dog at home – a doggy that can write emails on computer. Okay. I can enter into the spirit of things, if only to prove that I really do have a sense of humour. Better explain a few things first though:

1.   Where did you come from Lady Corrie-Rex Arabella Jayne?
2.   What in all that is seamanship is 'The Puppy Dog's Handbook' ?

3. How much did you cost me? Pedigree 'dawgs' with countless names never come cheap!
4. Dogmail.grrr What is this?
5. How quickly can I get rid of you? (Hee hee.)

I must admit though it's making my last few days on board more interesting. Can't wait to see you all again and tell you how much I have missed you. Hope the leaves are on the trees…
Regards

Nick er Daddy – now I am getting confused!

 Reply from: Corrie Jayne@dogmail.grrr

Outrageous is right. I found it under **O** in 'The Puppy Dog's Handbook'. Dogs can get very offended by their owners calling them by unsuitable names and Fur Face is definitely one of them. Bit a hole in your nice sweater just to make my feelings known – then took it out to the garden.

I write to inform you that I buried it in a big hole nicely dug by my good self, whilst Masie was watching TV and Nonnie was cleaning up before Mrs P the cleaning lady arrived. I also found the word *Offended* in the book and my Granpappy has very definite views on how a doggy should cope. I decided to turn my back on all humoans this morning and spent a good hour sulking in my boffin. Everyone thought it was because Nonnie scolded me for digging in the garden and then running into the kitchen. The floor was newly washed. I skidded along the hall and knocked over the flower arrangement on that silly pedestal by the door. I ended up with a carnation tucked into my ear and an eye full of water – very tiresome for a baby dog. Then Mrs P arrived to inspect. She laughed and said I was a sorry sight, and Nonnie and Masie laughed at me too. It's been one of those days.

But dear Daddy, I digrrrress – I really logged on to answer the questions you asked. No 1: Where did I come from? My dearrrr fellow, don't you know anything about dawgs? I am a Highlander, born and bred in the Scottish mountains bordering the Great Glen. That is my home. I could send a copy of my lineage as an attachment but I am afraid it would overload all the ship's 'puters. So, I am sending you a pretty Highland scene instead. It's a winter one from the day I was born. Brrrrrr.

My Happy Highland Home

Wagging tail – I am the only daughter of Marmaduke of Munlochy. He would have succeeded to the title of Chieftain of all Westies Near and Far, but he and my Mammy the dearest and sweetest of us all, Lady Bonny Heather of the Great Glen, were snatched by the Wicked Dog Rustlers o' MacNabbit when I was just a wee baby dog. They were taken far away over the Waters of Doom and never heard of again. My Granpappy was heartbroken and spent many a lonely night howling across the black waters - but they never answered his call.

Of course, I would like to point out that my Granpappy was no ordinary Westie. He was none other than Chieftain MacVic o' Kerrowdown an' Drum, Great Howler of the Mountains and Lord of the Great Glen, the Wisest of All the Westies. It was such an honour to be taken in by the Great Leader himself. Many a night I slept in my own wee boffin (a Scottish dog basket to you) next to his by the fireside. Oh Daddy! the stories he told, his wisdom, his juicy bone collection. I can see it all even as I write.

More later - it's my teatime. Tucker has not improved. If there is anything worse than Doggy Biccies, it's Doggy Meatie Hunks (dreadful smell, worse taste). But never mind, I have a plan...

Woof woofs
Corrie

| From: | EE NP Kent@MV.Welfordia Bay |
| To: | Nonnie@home.uk |

Just got in from watch. What has happened to my best sweater? I shall need an instant replacement – in lucky green, my favourite. I always said that pedestal flower arranging nonsense in the hall was a nightmare. I have knocked it over many a time and had to bribe Mrs P, the Cleaning Lady with the Aching Back and a Liking for Dust, with an extra cup of tea and a chocolate biscuit to sort it out before you arrived home from your art studio. I am beginning to have a sneaky regard for that dog. Should be turning for home tonight – will send my flight details once we get to Rotterdam.

Love you
Nick xxx

 Reply from: Mrs Nonnie Kent@home.uk

What is all this? How did you learn about Corrie, our new addition to the household? I was going to tell you when I spoke to you on the phone last week. But, I thought I would wait until you saw her for yourself. I know you do not like dogs, but Grandee brought her here for Masie. He said he felt sure you would adore her just as we do. She is very cute – well most of the time. She has had a B A D (Beastly Awful Dog) day today. She chewed your Lucky Green Golfing Sweater, and then buried it in the garden. Poor Grandee, he had just set out some really pretty primroses under the willow tree – Corrie dug them up and put them in a neat pile, then buried your sweater there instead. I was surprised how deep the hole was, she is such a tiny dog. Of course, Grandee was very cross. He chased Corrie all around the garden. Corrie ran into the kitchen just as Mrs P had finished cleaning the floor. Mud everywhere. Such screaming and yelling from Mrs P! Corrie ran along the hall, skidded and toppled my beautiful spring flower arrangement on the pedestal by the door. I had just completed it and I guess I was yelling too. Masie started to cry and Corrie hid under the stairs – she was all wet and had a carnation stuck in her ear. Grandee came in huffing and puffing like an old steam train and Mrs P was complaining about her back in that very loud voice she has. I nearly hid under the stairs, too. Anyway, Grandee put on the kettle and made the tea, Mrs P put the pedestal in the garage and I re-arranged the flowers in the beautiful vase Emiline bought me last Christmas. They look really nice. Masie found some chocolate biscuits and we all calmed down a bit – you know, 'Out with Anger, in with Love' that sort of thing. But, the poor little dog just sat in her basket all day with her back to us. She seemed most offended!!!

Fun and games at supper time, though. I had invited Grandee and Emiline over as it was fish pie – Masie's favourite. Corrie went mad! After sulking all day in her basket with her back to us, she jumped up and started doing silly tricks – begging and whining and chasing her tail. Grandee said I should give her some of the fish pie instead of the Doggie Meatie Hunks the vet recommended. She loved it – ate every bit instead of hiding it under the rug by the fire as she does with the Hunks. Then she jumped up on Grandee's lap, gave him a huge lick across his cheek, snuggled up and went to sleep. Guess it's time for me to snuggle up too – not many more days now and then you will be home.

Masie is watching the trees in the garden like a hawk, she says the leaves are beginning to grow!

Miss you
N xxx

From: Corrie Jane@dogmail.grrr
To: EE NP Kent@MV.Welfordia Bay

Dear Daddy

At last the 'puter's free! I thought Nonnie would never get to bed. Well, the plan worked, Daddy – found it under Cunning Plans in 'The PDH' as we Westies call Chieftain MacVic's book. Worked like a charm: all I had to do was a few Highland Flings across the dining room and I was rewarded with fish pie, my Highland favourite. My Granpappy and I used to share one every Tuesday night when I was a wee baby dog. Westies love Tuesdays!!!

Nonnie has told you the full story about today's adventure. I did not tell you the BAD bits – a dawg likes to make a good impression. It's all in the Handbook you know, which neatly brings me to your question (No: 2) about it. Well, Daddy, as I have already told you, I was taken in by my Granpappy MacVic, who even by humoan years was a very old dawg, when I was just a babe. He worried about me dreadfully. Who would pass on the great wisdom seen in every good Westie's eyes if he had the Last Calling before I was grown? It troubled him soooo much. He would spend hours just staring into the embers of the evening fire wondering what to do.

One sunny Sunday morning as we were looking out over the loch to the little village beyond, the answer came: the sound of bells carried on the breeze over the water. 'It's a sign,' MacVic growled and he trotted off home with his tail straight up in the air like a flag. I was very puzzled. What had he seen? Silly me – he had not seen anything at all – just heard the bells calling the humoans to church for singing and listening to stories. Granpappy set to work right away and with his own big muddy paws wrote 'The Puppy Dog's Handbook', the best doggy storybook of all. He filled it with everything Vital for Westies to Know Before Going A-travellin' with Their New Owners.

It was MacVic's legacy to all Westiekind and every puppy dog has a copy tucked away in their back pocket – presented to them by the Chief of All Westies before they go. MacVic knew he would not always be on hand to help us baby dogs – but his wisdom carrrrries on for ever.

Woof woofs
Corrie

 Reply from: EE NP Kent@MV.Welfordia Bay

Hello Fur Face

Sounds like you have had quite a day. Not done so good myself recently – bad weather over the Atlantic and the Welfordia Bay has been rocking and rolling. I fell down the poop deck steps to make matters worse and really hurt my back. I could out-do Mrs P at the moment! Hope it is better for our first walkies across the fields. Thank you for the photograph of your Highland Home – it's a very beautiful place. I have printed it off and put it on my desk. I am intrigued by 'The PDH' – I could do with one of those myself. It must be nice to know what to do in any given situation – good old MacVic! Glad you enjoyed your supper. I think you are keeping us all on our toes. What are the answers to the rest of my questions? I am enjoying this!!! Can't believe I am writing letters to a dog!

Daddy

Hello Nick

Not long to go before the end of your trip. Thought I would just pen you a few lines to update you. Masie is growing all the time and looks more like her Mummy every day – not that I am biased, mind! Nonnie is well but works too hard – too many ideas and not enough canvas! Emiline is still into keep fit and healthy eating, even though her apple dumplings are to die for (bad for this old boy's waistline – but who cares).

Of course, I have put my foot in it all round. Bought a little dog from the Poor Doggy Rescue Centre in Harborough last week. Could not resist her – a little West Highland White Terrier just like the one I had when I was a boy. As you know, I lived in Scotland, and the times that wee dog and I had chasing over the heather. I thought that Masie would love to have a doggy like her. We have christened her Corrie – named after my own boyhood pet. Sorry lad, the dog is causing havoc just like wise old Emiline said she would. Uprooted all the plants I put in yesterday and buried your Lucky Green Sweater under the tree. Then she knocked over the plant stand in the hall. Mrs P had a pink fit and Nonnie was appealing to everyone to stop shouting while doing most of it herself!

At supper, Corrie decided she wanted a share of the fish pie we were eating and played up until she got some. But she went off to bed quite happily afterwards, wagging her tail.

Nonnie has told me that you do not like dogs. Just give Corrie a chance, **please** – she is a rascal I admit – but very loyal and loving and she will be a nice little friend for

Masie. Corrie badly needs a good home, Nick, she has had a rough time of it. Well enough pleading – see you soon. Would you like me to pick you up at the airport?

Regards

Grandee
PS Emiline sends her love.

From: Corrie Jane@dogmail.grrr
To: EE NP Kent@MV.Welfordia Bay

Dear Daddy

Here is a letter – despite the continued use of the term Fur Face!!! I think Grandee is on to me... he keeps on telling me he knows my little tricks. Surely he has not caught me writing to you? A doggy must be brave and true, so I will continue.

Thank you for your email. I hope that your back is better. You must pick up your paws more carefully my dear, or we will not get those walkies. In answer to the last three questions:

No 3: How much did I cost? Well, let me tell you, Westies of my pedigree are very often priceless. Westies do not discuss money, my dear fellow, it's not polite – and you do not need a handbook to know that. I have been installed at Wishing Well House, Millennium Drive for Very Special Reasons. One day, that will be clear to you.

No 4: And what is wrong with dogmail.grrr? It's a very useful email address, especially for a Westie's use. Best of all – it's free!!!

No 5: How do you get rid of me? That is a very nasty question and one that deserves a bite on the heel. May I remind you that I was invited to be Man's Best Friend in your house by Grandee himself – only he can get rid of me, as you so rudely put it, because he understands the Special Reasons for my being here.

Now I have a question of my own:

When are you coming home? We are all very excited here. The leaves are just poking through on the willow tree in the garden. I have found the very spot where I buried your Lucky Green Sweater and Masie has been very busy making a Welcome Home banner with Emiline– but DO act surprised when you see it. As for Nonnie – she has been to the hairdressers, and has bought herself a new dress as well, to wear when she picks you up from the airport with Grandee.

So, To-da-looooooo until we meet at last.

Corrie

From:	EE NP Kent@MV.Welfordia Bay
To:	Grandee@greenhouse.is my office

Hello Grandee, you old rascal.

Thank you for the email – so it's you sending me the emails from Corrie@dogmail.grrr. I think they are very funny and I am really looking forward to meeting the furry hound. I realize she must be a wonderful dog and bought for Special Reasons – all of which we can discuss when I get back. I am sure she will be good for Masie. I don't really hate dogs, it's just that I know nothing about them, as I have never had a dog before. However, walking her across the fields to the canal should be lots of fun.

I hope to be home next Wednesday on the 8.30am flight, will phone later with the flight number, so tell Nonnie to wait up.

Love to Emiline

Nick

 Reply from: Grandee@greenhouse.is my office.

Nick – what is all this dogmail.grrr nonsense? I really do not know what you are talking about and I certainly have not been sending you emails from Corrie. I think you have been working far too hard and need the break! It is good news that you are prepared to give the wee dog a chance though. I am very relieved. See you on Wednesday.

Grandee

FOLDER TWO

Subject: A Doggy Bids You Welcome!

	From:	Corrie Jayne@dogmail.grrr
	To:	EE NP Kent@home.uk

Dear Daddy

Here I am, sitting patiently in the office next to the PC. I will wait here all day in the hope that you will pick up this email and write back to me.

Welcome Home!

Your very own Baby Dog
The Lady Corrie-Rex Arabella Jayne o' Kerrowdown an' Drum

Baby Dog? The Lady Corrie-Rex Arabella Jayne o' Kerrowdown an' Drum?? Welcome Home??? You fierce barking Poochette! This is Daddy calling. I still can't figure out who is sending me this doggy stuff – but watch out when I am feeling less tired and stressed and this humoan WILL WORK IT OUT.

So, Lady Corrie-Rex Arabella Jayne – I saw you sitting by the desk in the office and thought I would switch on the computer and log onto my home email address, to see if there were any messages. Surprise! There was a letter from you. So this is how we communicate while I am home, is it?

Welcome Home – some welcome, you furry attacker. Brave Heart himself could not have improved on it. All I could see hurtling towards me was a white blur growling in fury. I did not even have time to clamber back inside the taxi before you launched yourself at my chest, knocking me completely off balance. Goodness knows what the neighbours thought – all that terrible growling and barking while I lay flat on my back in the only puddle in the street. Poor Nonnie, dressed only in her bathrobe and her long dark hair all wet from rushing out of the shower, hastily tried to get the situation under control and pulled you off me at last. Masie was crying. The taxi driver was no help, demanding his money in that surly way and then not giving me any change.

I am shocked! After all the assurances Grandee gave me that you were a Perfectly Behaved Dog, I was met by a Wild Thing. I blame myself, of course, should have known better. After all, you are from a DOG HOME. Let me tell you, Lady Muck, that a dog is supposed to be Man's Best Friend. My nerves had already been shot to bits by that fool taxi driver – rushing down the motorway with scant regard for speed limits or other road users. I really did not need to be met on my own driveway by a roaring lion in disguise.

Then the final insult: Nonnie is yelling at you that DADDY'S ARRIVED and the barking suddenly stops. There is a terrible silence AND THEN you WEE all over my shoes!!! Too angry to write more.

Daddy!!!

 Reply from: Corrie Jayne@dogmail.grrr

Well, Daddy, we seem to have got off on the wrong paws, I admit that. BUT, you sneaked home a day *earlier* than expected. A doggy can surely be forgiven (and bought an extra juicy bone) for making a few little errors of judgement at our first meeting.

Wagging tail, you should be proud of me. I was merely trying out my Anti Burglar Tactics as set down by my Granpappy in 'The PDH'.

1.   Be on guard at all times for tall thin strangers in scruffy clothes.
2.   Bark and growl fiercely, while watching to see if they appear scared.
3.   Launch The Attack using a running growl and knock 'em over.
4.   Once they are frozen to the spot in terror, wee on shoes to let 'em know who is boss.

Carried out to the letter! Granpappy would be proud. I'm not so sure he would be proud of you, Daddy. How silly you looked scrambling back into the taxi. You were covered in mud and shouting for me to be put on my lead. Westies hate leads. Unless it is for a proper walkies, it is deemed an indignity, and I did not deserve that after rescuing the family from an intruder. Everyone was shouting and our Masie was crying. The driver demanded an extra tenner for messing up his nice clean car and you lost your temper with everyone. What a rotten start to your vacation. You were trying to surprise us – and in the end we surprised you!!! I really feel for you – and you *can* pat me and I promise not to scare you again.

However, let us get something straight once and for all, Daddy. I was taken in by the *Poor Doggy Rescue Centre* because I was homeless through no fault of my own. It can happen to anyone. I have had a very bad time of it, I can tell you, and I am looking forward to living in a nice settled home again with a loving family who absolutely ADORE ME. When you can demonstrate that I am indeed ADORED I shall let you tickle my tummy. Until then, I shall sleep in Masie's room – and neither Masie nor I will come out until you say that you are sorry.

LCJ

PS For your information, the next door neighbours moved out the day before I arrived – I think we are getting new ones next Friday.

From:	Grandee@greenhouse.is my office
To:	NP Kent@home.uk

Hello Nick

I have just had a visit from the Postie. Your homecoming is the talk of the village. Nick, that doggy is utterly fearless. I am so glad. She will see that the whole family will come to no harm. What a Brave Highland Lassie she is! Glad you made it through your own front door at last, despite Nonnie's, Corrie's and Masie's best efforts to leave you on the steps. I knew they would see sense in the end.

Thanks for the whisky – Nonnie dropped it off on her way to the studio. I had a little word with her about your tantrum and she saw the funny side and went back to let you in. I am sure she will be speaking to you by tonight.

Thanks also for letting me off Airport Duty – it would have been a very early start for me. See you later when the jet lag has worn off and the dust has settled.

Grandee

From: NP Kent@home.uk
To: Corrie Jayne@dogmail.grrr

Okay, Corrie, you can come out of hiding in Masie's room. You are forgiven!!! Nonnie is speaking to me again after I went to *Pat's Flowers* and just about bought the entire stock. Nonnie loves flowers – and watch out because the pedestal has been brought in from the garage.

I know that you and Masie spent the entire morning playing with the puzzles and dolls I brought from Japan. Nonnie has taken the whisky to Grandee, Mrs P with the Aching Back and a Liking for Dust is busy trying to break the vacuum cleaner, and I am in the office and all is right with my world. Emiline is fixing supper. It's the Big Family Dinner, a copy of the one I missed when I was away. You can have some 'humoan' food tonight – but I want to see your Highland Fling first. Then Grandee and I will open up a bottle o' whisky from my secret store, and we will mull over your pedigree. In the meantime – I am just off to get that juicy bone you ordered and take my crumpled muddy clothes to the cleaners. I always wear comfy stuff to travel in, as the journey back from a ship is usually a long one. Why am I writing this to a DOG?

Daddy

 Reply from: Corrie Jayne@dogmail.grrr

Dear Daddy

Thank you for my juicy bone and for the unexpected gift of a nice new tartan collar. Clan MacDog, if I am not mistaken. It looks so well against my gleaming white fur. I shall wear it with pride. Okay, so I spent the afternoon peering at my reflection in the fish pond. Dogs do that sort of thing. My new collar looks so well on me – I am sure I can be forgiven for acting the Pawfectly Posh Dawg and walking up and down the driveway with my nose in the air. I am now off to the garden again to chew on my juicy bone and I promise not to bury it with your Lucky Green Sweater when I have done. Nonnie loved the flowers you bought her and I could hardly stop prancing when I saw how you kissed her. Oh Daddy!

Woofs and hearts...

Corrie

Good Day Doggy!!! It's Wednesday and a fine clear day, unlike Grandee's head, after drinking all that whisky. I had to take the man home last night! Emiline was very cross with both of us – nothing new there then!

It was a great evening. You did well at the Doggy Dancing – Grandee was so impressed. He thought I had spent the afternoon teaching you to do the Fling – decided not to admit that I fell asleep watching the golf on TV.

I have been thinking. If you are a magical doggy, it's high time that you stopped looking at your reflection in the fish pond and told me a little more of your story. I would especially like an explanation of your behaviour this morning, little family dog.

It had started so well. My nice new car arrived promptly at nine o'clock and Masie and I decided to take it for a spin. Picked Grandee up from his house in Lime Tree Road at nine-thirty as planned. Decided to take you with me as dogs love caries, beats walkies every time, according to Masie, and off we went. Grandee was sporting his tartan waistcoat. I wonder if he knows he is wearing the MacDog Tartan? Masie found a Bay City Rollers CD to play and a very merry trip it promised to be.

How pretty the spring hedgerows looked in the sunlight as the new car purred along the country lanes. I even started to like the Bay City Rollers music – but don't tell Nonnie, as I have teased her about the band for years.

It was on the way home, little family doggy, that things started to go wrong. Grandee only wanted to show you off at the *Poor*

Doggy Rescue Centre. All that crying and howling – I was embarrassed. Then, you hid under the seat and refused to come out. Masie started to cry (again) and poor old Grandee got stuck when he tried to pull you out. He really should go on a diet!

Why did you kick up such a fuss? Was it because of the photographs of you on the wall in Reception? I must admit I hardly recognized you, poor little mite, so thin, and your coat all shaggy and bedraggled. What in all that is seamanship happened to you? Your little paws had been bleeding from walking so far. I was shocked.

So, now that you have enjoyed a nice steak lunch along with the rest of us – stop snoozing in your boffin and tell me the story.

Daddy

 Reply from: Corrie Jayne@dogmail.grrr

Dear Daddy

A little doggy gets verrrrry scared sometimes. Memories are not always happy. What was I to think when our lovely outing ended at the *Poor Doggy Rescue Centre*? I decided not to leave the safety of our nice new car – in case you left me there. It's a nice place – but not as nice as my new home. I love my new address: Wishing Well House, Millennium Drive. It sounds so classy, much like me. Pawfect for a baby dog. I felt sooo let down – especially after the fun evening we had spent together.

It reminded me of the evenings I spent with my dear lost Mammy and Daddy when I was just a wee babe. Emiline is a super cook. Great tucker – much appreciated by all. We wolfed it down and everyone loved my Fling!!! I went to my boffin a tad on the full side!

Everyone sat at the table after dinner, just talking, and the groanups played cards. Even Masie was allowed to stay up as it's half-term. We shared a hand between us – could have won, too, if Grandee had not 'found' a spare ace under the table! It was an evening filled with laughter and fun – a proper family evening.

I felt at home at last – you know, that special warm glow inside mixed from firelight, good food and jolly company – it's not often found in a humoan's lair, I can tell you. But life can play cruel tricks on a doggy, and a Westie is always on guard.

I know that today's outing started so well and dogs *love* caries. The new car in Loch Ness Silver is very fine – and I was feeling every inch the Posh Dawg. But when we pulled up outside the *Poor Doggy Rescue Centre* I was in shock. I could smell the despair of the dogs inside even before we rounded the corner.

So, I cried and hid under the seat, just in case the outing was a trick to send me back there. 'Always be alert to any dangers,' my Granpappy used to say. A baby dog could not be sure, and I remembered what you had written about getting rid of me, little ME, in your email, so I refused to move. Westies do that sort of thing very well, I think. It's called Making a Statement Without Uttering a Word. Works every time. Pity Grandee got stuck between the seats trying to force me out. He should have known better at his age.

However, my doggy licks on his nose soon got him moving again. Glad you went in without me. Howled at all my friends in the Rescue Centre from the safety of the driver's seat and admired my reflection in the wing mirrors. Think I could do with a cushion though, Daddy – then I can see over the steering wheel properly.

Woof woofs
Corrie

 Reply from: NP Kent@home.uk

Corrie, it's 3am and I have been watching carefully to see when you nip into the office and email me on the computer. Nonnie is getting worried about me. She keeps looking at me with those big grey eyes of hers and I can see pity in them. I am feeling a lot less tired, my furry friend, and I will find out who is sending me the doggy stuff. In the meantime, please answer the questions from our previous correspondence – and keep off the driver's seat in the new car. It's covered in doggy biccies and little balls of mud off your feet and we have only had it two days.

Daddy

 Reply from: Corrie Jayne@dogmail.grrr

Nonnie is indeed getting worried about you. I heard her discussing it with Mrs P today. Of course, Mrs P blames the long sea trips and all that salty air. Apparently the sea plays tricks on a person. I feel exactly the same about bath-time. Dogs hate bath-time and it was too bad of you to bath me this morning. I had just finished burying my bone and was feeling rather pleased with my efforts. You crept up on me, called me a good doggy, then whisked me into the bathroom.

Most unfair. I was covered in Woof and Go and my fur lathered up like Mrs P's dish mop. Gleaming fur is one thing – trying to be a model dog is not a Westie's style. I like being mucky now and then!!! More later when I have finished sulking in my boffin.

Lady Corrie Jayne CD (Clean Dog)

From:	Nonnie@art studio.paint
To:	NP Kent@home.uk

Hello Nick

I will be a bit late getting home. I'm in the middle of a painting and you know how it is when inspiration hits! Hope your morning has gone well. Did you have fun bathing Corrie?

N xxx

Reply from: NP Kent@home.uk

Hello Darling

Thanks for your email. Come on, Nonnie – is it you sending me the doggy stuff? I know you love the rascally pooch – I have quite a sneaky regard for her myself – but you need not have gone to such extreme lengths to ensure that I accept her as part of the Kent Family of Wishing Well House.

Yes, I bathed Corrie. She hated it – and is now sulking in her boffin. She has pulled it right under the stairs. Here is a photo. Hope she cheers up soon; she is better at black looks than you are!

I am cooking supper tonight, so be warned! I always know when the food is cooked when the smoke alarm goes off in the hall!!!

Love you
Nick XXXXX

 Reply from: Nonnie@art studio.paint

Nick – what is all this Doggy Stuff you are talking about? I promise you it is not me sending you emails from Corrie. My money would be on Grandee... You know how much he loves a joke. Have you asked him? Supper sounds fun!!!

N xxx

Dear Daddy

We had such a lovely walkies this afternoon. It was such fun to run along the river bank and inspect all the newborn flowers. The violets are out – I love violets!!! And it really felt like spring.

You kept asking me about my earlier days while we were out. I cannot talk to you Daddy – I can only communicate via email. It is not Nonnie, Grandee, nor even Masie sending you the doggy stuff – it really is me, me, ME! Little ME!

So, here is some more of my story. It is about the time when I first left my Highland Homeland to start adventures with a new humoan family:

My dear, I could hardly wait. My pedigree documents were stamped, my paws and ears cleaned and then I was presented with my very own copy of 'The Puppy Dog's Handbook' Issue Number 1 signed *'With woofs and licks for a good life from Granpappy'*. I was ready to go!

I suppose there was many a Westie to envy the Chieftain's Girleen off on her Travels. The family who had chosen me were TOP DRAWER, I can tell you. Desmond and Winnie Mallory-Pickard-Watts and their two children Toby (age 10) and Fiona-Mia (age 12). Three homes – all five-star residences. One in London, one in Monte Carlo and one in the Scottish Highlands near Glen Affric. Of course, for all

Westies the most desired place is Glen Affric. It is a piece of heaven, a place of natural beauty, endless paths to follow by the fast flowing river, and spectacular scenery to do it in. My dearrrrrr – the Lady Corrie Jayne had *made it*. Granpappy was soooo proud.

How he growled under his breath with pleasure, as I was popped onto the back seat of their brand new Howldi GTi that gleamed in the sunshine. We were to go along the motorways to London; the adventure had begun. It was a pity the family was already running late. The journey took forever and I was sick on the leather seat. Winnie was HORRIFIED. My, how that woman could shout. Everyone else joined in. Then it got doggy-well worse – Desmond screeched the car to a halt and threw me into the boot. It was so dark and airless I thought I would die Daddy – I really did. Could not even see to read any good advice in my Handbook. But Westies are strong – and eventually we got to the big city. Noise, smell, fumes: a baby dog was very scared.

They had told lies, Daddy. The family lived in an apartment, not a big house with a nice view – or a garden for a doggy as they had promised. The apartment seemed to be all glass, chrome, and woodblock floors that made me skid. There was nowhere for me to play, just a service yard covered in concrete with a few dandelions peeping through in the corner. I was let out once a day – and if I did a whoopsie in between, everyone shouted at me. I was not very popular from Day One. The Mallory-Pickard-Watts only wanted a doggy as a fashion statement – and I made statements of a different kind. I did not even have a proper boffin – just a wire basket with a black cushion in. Designer, of course.

Soon the school term started and I was left alone for *hours*. Dogs hate that. One day I skidded right along the hallway while I was sniffing around looking for something to do, and 'The PDH' fell right out of my back pocket. I quickly picked it up. It was open at N – and N is for Novelty Value. My Granpappy had sent me A Sign.

'Once the Novelty Value of being the most wonderful member of the household has worn off, little Westie, beware. It may be that you will be neglected, left without food and warmth or worse... unloved. If it is all of these: ESCAPE. (Turn to E for Escape for more information.)
Granpappy'

More tomorrow, Daddy – it's getting light and Nonnie will soon be up and about. It's going to be a lovely day. Mrs P is taking me on a walkies to the village shop and that is always good for a choccy biccie as I wait for her outside.

Woof woofs
Corrie

 Reply from: NP Kent@home.uk

Corrie! How could you leave me on such a cliff-hanger. Inadvertently sent the doggy stuff to the *Welfordia Bay* and now everyone wants to know: WHAT HAPPENED NEXT? I have had a call from the Captain and you are going to be the ship's mascot – I am sending them some photographs of you. So hurry up and finish the story.

Daddy

Reply from: Corrie Jayne@dogmail.grrr

Dear Daddy and Ship's Crew

Wagging Tail! It's Lady Corrie-Rex Arabella Jayne o' Kerrowdown an' Drum. I have always wanted to have a fan club. But to be a ship's mascot is really an honour for Westies everywhere. Pawfect. Boys, note the proud set of my head and the alert stance with my ears in the air. Only the finest Westies in the whole wide world and Inverness have such a stance.

Wagging Tail
Corrie

 Reply from: NP Kent@home.uk

Never mind all that pedigree malarkey – on with the plot!

Daddy

 From: Nonnie@art studio.paint
To: NP Kent@home.uk

Nick

You are spending far too much time on the internet looking for emails from the dog. Here is a list of jobs you *PROMISED* to do when you came home – most of them are from last vacation.

Jobs List

1. Fix squeak on third step of the stairs.
2. Retune the TV, its all foggy.
3. Sort out your books – there are thousands in the office. Christine at *Bookworms* said she would take any spares and pay you. Masie is looking forward to the dosh for her next holiday.
4. Decorate the lounge – please!!!
5. There is a draught coming down the stairs from the loft – find and fix it.
6. Build a barbeque in the back garden.
7. Grandee says we need a garden shed. What do you think?
8. Holiday brochures – we need a break!

Nick, I am worried about the way you look at Corrie. You do like her, don't you? N xxx

---

From: Corrie Jayne@dogmail.grrr
To: NP Kent@home.uk

Dear Daddy

I have crept on tippy-paws into the office – avoiding all the books on the floor – to write to you this early sunny morn. Yesterday was another grrrrrreat day. Dogs love it when things are happy at home. I know I got a bit carried away, scurrying about and hiding the colour charts for the lounge – but it's a dog thing. A well-kept croft is always in demand. Now on with my tail – sorry – tale...

Here is an extract from 'The Puppy Dog's Handbook':
There are Four Pawsteps to Escape from Reality:

1. *Eat everything in sight afore ye go – as it may be a while before you find fresh tucker.*
2. *Plan the moment v carefully.*
3. *When the moment comes – don't look back.*
4. *Treat it as an adventure and remember:* **North is Home**.

Never-the-Ness (sorry, thinking about the Loch). Never-the-less, a well-brought-up Westie would never walk out on a TOP DRAWER family unless things were really bad. I decided to chew it over for a few days. Winnie's best pink shoes, Jimmy Chews, with the v high heels, seemed pawfect for the task. They reminded me so much of the sticks Granpappy kept under his boffin to chew and help clean his teeth. When Winnie came in that night she was utterly FURIOUS. She growled at me – her voice like Highland Thunder resounding o'er the Munro Mountains. I was v scared. She waved the chewy shoes in the air. She beat the mangled heels on the polished floor boards then chased me all over the apartment. Her face redder than her podgy feet, pounded along the wooden floors. Her bottle blonde hair stuck up in spikes – she looked like a haggis in a hurricane. Doggy Amazin'!

I skidded along the wooden floorboards and crashed into the CD rack, leaving a trail of doggy destruction behind me. (Hee hee.) I legged it into Toby's room and hid under his bed. Lots of smelly socks and left-overs on the floor – I could have camped out there for a week if needs be, while I thought how I could get away from this trrrrruly awful family.

Daddy dear, I would love to write more, but the Removing Van has arrived next door and I must investigate!

Corrie

34

FOLDER THREE

Subject: The Moving-in Day

From: Corrie Jayne@dogmail.grrr
To: NP Kent@home.uk

Dear Daddy

I have been looking out of the window all morning because the Removing Van has arrived at the house next door and goodies are being unloaded. Masie is standing at the gate with her bicycle and her friend, the little boy from two doors down. His name is Mani and his Daddy owns the Chinese Take-Away in Harborough called *Woks the Matter*.

They are looking to see what is going on. Grandee calls it 'Keeping Doggo', a term he learned years ago when he was far away in the Army. It means keeping a close watch on things and being alert.

I thought I would do much the same myself. Well, Daddy, all sorts of exciting things are going into the house. A comfy gold, three-piece suite, glass-topped coffee table on stumpy brass legs, a large standard lamp with a huge gold shade, beds and bedding and lots of things stacked up in tea chests. It's good to have a new beginning, I always say. But, it's a shame they are movin' in on a Friday. Mrs P keeps muttering 'Friday flitting not long sitting,' almost as though she dislikes the new arrivals already. I will reserve my best doggy judgement until I have met the new owners. In the meantime, I note that Garge and Micky, the removing men, have just unloaded the dining room table and chairs from the van. They look so well in the front garden especially now that Micky has put his Thermos flask of coffee on top and spread out his newspaper. Pawfect. What is this? He has just opened up his lunch box and I can spy a Tunnock's Caramel Choccy Biccie – my Highland favourite.

Wagging tails...
Corrie

 Reply from: NP Kent@home.uk

Wish I had read your email before you galloped into next door's garden. How you cleared our gates was worthy of an Olympic medal! Poor Micky and Garge the removal men were terrified as you leapt onto the dining table, upset the flask of coffee all over the racing pages of Micky's paper, and nose-dived their lunch box. I thought you were a civilised dog. How you chased them around the lawn yapping and barking! I was embarrassed, especially as the new neighbours turned up just as you pinned Micky up against the oak tree in their back garden. He had to pacify you with his chocolate bar. Nonnie and I made amends by offering coffee and sandwiches to everyone, including Grandee who had just popped in to see Masie and ask how Keeping Doggo was going. Where were you? On guard? No! Keeping Doggo for Grandee? No! You were wolfing down the chocolate bar, stretched out under the Norton's dining table without a care in the world.

I must say the new neighbours seem rather nice. Quality, in fact. I am sure we will be good friends. He is a well-groomed something in the City and she is… rather stunning. We have never had an ex-model living next door before. The Blonde Bombshell, Grandee called her – behind her back, of course. Things are definitely looking up in Millennium Drive.

Daddy!

 Reply from: Corrie Jayne@dogmail.grrr

Dear Daddy

Roll up your tongue! That woman next door cannot hold a candle to our dear Nonnie. Not only is Nonnie the kindest, sweetest most sonsie (meaning beautiful and clever) lassie in the whole world, Daddy, she is also very long suffering. That woman next door has a CAT name of General Woo Woo (hee hee, silly name even for a Siamese pedigree moggy) and both of them have sharp and nasty claws. So watch out! I myself will be Keeping Catto for a very long time to come.

It has been quite an eventful day really and I am doggy exhausted. Micky and Garge have left me a whole box of Tunnock's Caramels after they decided to back a horse called The Wagster in the 4.30pm at Hey Dog Bark. It romped home at 25 to 1, whatever that means. They are really in the money and so are the new neighbours, Grandee and yourself. Glad you decided to take Nonnie out to dinner tonight. She looked soooooo beautiful in the floating heather-coloured dress you bought her.

Thank you for the doggie bag of goodies you brought back from the restaurant for me. Sorry I could not touch a thing. Felt a bit sick after all those choccy biccies. Might be off my food for a few days, Daddy – watching my figure!!!

To-da-loooo
Corrie

From: Grandee@greenhouse.is my office
To: NP Kent@home.uk

Hello Nick

Just been going through the racing pages for tomorrow. Cannot see any doggy stuff at Haydock Park, but will keep you posted. Hope Corrie is okay. She stayed in her boffin all night with her eyes tight shut, which is not like her.

Masie was a good girl – put herself to bed with the new story books I bought her. We all had a good time today and it has ended with a profit. That little dog is a fine Westie. Fancy Micky spotting The Wagster in the racing pages. He thought Corrie had given him a sign when she wagged her tail for the biscuit he gave her. And the rest is history.

So glad that you are becoming good friends wi' the wee doggy – she is a real asset to the family and no mistake. See you tomorrow!

Grandee

From: Masie@playtime.is best

To: NP Kent@home.uk

Helo Daddy. I no that Cori emales u an I want her to rite to me too. so will u ask her to pleze? I am lernin aboot lettas an emales at skool so I thought I would send u a practise emale. Mummy sez she likes lettars in the post best as long as they are not Bill's. Who is Bill? Had a great day today Daddy with Mani. WE rode our bikes and kept Doggo on wot went into the Nortuns house. Mani thinks they are v snobby. Did Corrie keep Doggo? Is that y she is 2 tired to bark tonite Daddy?

Love Masie

Reply from: NP Kent@home.uk

Masie, thank you for your email. I know it is not you writing the doggy stuff to me as your spelling needs attention. Have you had a lesson on spell check at school yet? Otherwise, it was a very good letter and I am proud of you for your first attempt. I agree it would be better if Corrie emailed you, it would be a good fairy story – but she has chosen me for the time being. By the way, Mummy does not mean that Bill is a person – she means bill as in settling money that is owed.

That little dog has been sent to us for Special Reasons,

according to Grandee. It may even be that she was sent to make us rich and then it does not matter how many bills we get – they can all be paid. We all won money on The Wagster so who knows what will happen next.

I am sure Corrie will be fine tomorrow – one choccy biccie too many, I think – which will keep her in bed and off my computer for the time being.

Sleep tight and with love from

Daddy xxxxx

 From: NP Kent@home.uk
To: Corrie Jayne@dogmail.grrr

It's Saturday...

Earth to Corrie
Earth to Corrie
Come in, please...

Daddy

 From: NP Kent@home.uk
To: Corrie Jayne@dogmail.grrr

It's Sunday...

Earth to Corrie
Earth to Corrie
Come in, please...

Daddy

| From: | NP Kent@home.uk |
| To: | Corrie Jayne@dogmail.grrr |

It's Monday…

Earth to Corrie
Earth to Corrie
Come in, please...

I know that you have been a poorly dog all weekend and this morning I will take you to the Vet. I am so worried about you, little family doggy. You have hardly opened your eyes in two days and you keep whimpering in your sleep. Please tell me, what is wrong?

Daddy

| From: | NP Kent@home.uk |
| To: | Nonnie@art studio.paint |

Hello Nonnie Darling

Hope your day is going well. I am so pleased that you are in the running for designing a mural for the new *le Woodlands* restaurant in town. I did not know that our new neighbours, Rexxie and Angelica Norton, have taken it on as a new business venture to add to his City Portfolio, whatever that means! It was so nice of them to approach you to submit some ideas.

I took Corrie to the Vet this morning as she was sick in the garden twice after you left and could hardly lap from her water bowl. The Vet gave her the VIP (Very Important Poochette) treatment and all was going well until the injection came out. Corrie was not having any of that. Growled like fury. I was a bit scared she would bite. However, she was too weak to do anything really and took it like a good dog. She has picked up an infection – probably from drinking canal water when we were on our walkies. The Vet is keeping her in today and putting her on a drip. She looked very frail, I must say. If you want to call in on your way home the Vet says you are welcome. I am not taking Masie in as I don't want to upset her.

See you later
Nick xxxx

From:	Corrie Jayne@dogmail.grrr
To:	NP Kent@home.uk

Dear Daddy

I hope you and Nonnie have a pawfectly good reason for leaving me behind at the Vet's of all places. I have had a dreadful time of it. I will never experiment with canal water again and I very well might give up choccy biccies as well. Dreadful Vet – practising his drip insertions on a poor sick doggy, an' worse; keeping me in Puppy Dog Intensive Care for almost a week. Now I am to take tablets the size of golf balls. I have swallowed one of them this morning – but not without a fight. Vettie has agreed to let me come home and here I am at last. I need to be on a light diet for a whole week, rice an' chicken – BORING!!! I need a bath, Daddy, as I smell rather pongo-wiffity, but not today, I beg you. I also have two plasters on my paws where the drip has been – these need to come off. So if you are into Yung Foo Fighting, I can show you a few moves while you try to remove them (hee hee).

Promise to be quite good for you – and thank you for getting me better, even though I have had nasty dreams all the while I was at the Vet's. I expect I was doggy delirious.
Woof woofs,
Lady Corrie-Rex Arabella Jayne o' Kerrowdown an' Drum (excess wee on a Thursday and soiler of carpets extraordinairrrrrre)

WESTIES LOVE SCOTLAND AND I WANT TO GO HOME!!! GRRrrrrrrrrrr. PAWFECT PLACE FOR RECUPERRRRRRATION.

 Reply from: NP Kent@home.uk

Thank you for the email. Glad to know that you are feeling better. Please – no more wees or whoopsies on the carpets – Nonnie is trying to sting me for new ones throughout the house and making you the excuse. What is all this about a trip to Scotland? I suppose we could manage a week or so, providing there is no more howling in your sleep at night. Whatever is the matter with you?

Daddy

 Reply from: Corrie Jayne@dogmail.grrr

Dear Daddy

What is wrong? Bad memories. That is what is wrong. Started when I was doggy delirious – started remembering my life before I came to Millennium Drive and the time I

43

was first away from my Highland Home. Oh Daddy! I just want to go home to Scotland – it's a Westie promise I made to myself when I lived in London with my First Family. Here is a photograph of Haggis, my favourite Highland Cow. She always knew when it was milking time and trotted along the road all by herself each evening to the milking parlour. She knew how to get home – now I need the knowledge, too. There is nothing in 'The Puppy Dog's Handbook' and the instructions Granpappy gave me were not enough. 'Remember, North is Home'. Well, that saying got me into all sorts of a doggy mess.

You remember you were asking about my adventures? Well, here is the next instalment. I have already told you I was looking to Escape – as per the instructions in 'The PDH'...

Before I did, I wanted to be sure there was no hope that I would ever fit in. Westies are very loyal, you know. I used to dream that I would win first prize in a Dog Show, my fur gleaming and my pedigree details dancing in the breeze behind me as I was given my rosette. Surely then my First Family would doggy adore me? I waited to see if they would enter me in proper dog shows, like a Match Meeting, or even a Limit Show, as my Granpappy told me they would. It was not to be. I doubt that they even knew the value of such shows. The Chieftain's Lassie would never get the chance to win the Clootie Dumpling Award.

Then came the moment, when I really was certain that I was not loved. It came on a wet Wednesday. I was in my wire boffin, having spent the past night and day under Toby's bed until things calmed down again. I was idly scratching an itch in my fur. Winnie saw me and was convinced I had a flea. She was sooooo wrong!!! I just needed a bath-time as my fur was too long and getting matted. Of course, everyone started to scratch an imaginary itch – even permanently scruffy Toby, who thought it was all a huge joke. The *Rid-a-Bug Pest Control Agency* was immediately called out and soon the whole apartment was drenched in spray. I thought I would die from the fumes – then suddenly I was whisked away in my wire boffin down the marble staircase to the service yard and dumped amongst the rubbish with the chewed shoes. Me, little ME, abandoned. How could they do such a thing? I was pawfectly embarrassed and sure at last that my time to Escape had come. I was soooo sad. Who would believe my proud pedigree once I had left the paperwork behind? I would just be another waif and stray trying to find her way in the big wide world.

It was v cold out there all alone in the dark. Then the dawn came, and suddenly the refuse collection lorry roared into the service yard. Before I knew what had happened, my wire boffin was gobbled up with the rest of the rubbish. Then I saw the gate was open, Daddy – and I just slipped away.

Nonnie is calling me – it's time for a dreaded pill. She is always game for a bit of Yung Foo Fighting. More later.

Corrie

Hello Doggo!

Glad you are feeling well enough to play us up today. I know that you always put your tummy first – but correction here: it is not Yung Foo Fighting it's Kung Foo Fighting – and has nothing to do with growling and running up and down the stairs with Nonnie in hot pursuit. Thank you for your email. I am enjoying your story and so are the Captain and crew of the *Welfordia Bay*. I would love to hear another instalment when you have a few minutes to yourself. How about tonight? The Nortons are coming around for drinkies at 8pm and I want to make a good impression – so if you were quietly composing the next chapter of your adventure it would be much to your advantage.

I really like the idea of a few days in Scotland. It could tie in with our plans quite well. Nonnie has been approached by Rexxie to submit designs for a big picture to be painted on the wall of his new *le Woodlands* restaurant. It's what is known as a mural. It's to be of a woodland with a river and mountains in the background. Scotland would be the perfect place for sketching – so take your tablets like a good dog and we can be away at Masie's half term. I hope Rexxie will like the sketches Nonnie is submitting for approval. Keep your paws crossed!

Daddy

Hi Nick

Sounds like you are having an eventful vacation. We have just docked in Houston. Chief Mate found a lovely dog collar in the *Cutie Pie Pet Store* just up the road. We are sending it on express delivery for Lady Corrie-Rex Arabella Jayne. We thought she might need cheering up after being so poorly.

Captain & Crew

PS Send on the latest instalment of her story. We had no idea you could write stories. You are really keeping us entertained!!!

Reply from: NP Kent@home.uk

Hello lads

Yes, my vacation is going well, but flying by – only six weeks to go and I will be back on board for another trip. I have not found out who sends me the doggy emails yet. Nonnie is too busy, Grandee can only think about horse racing, Masie cannot spell and I could not write such a tail – sorry – tale! Here is Corrie's next instalment written in the dead of night with her own muddy paws! I know that she will swank in her 'diamond' collar. Thank you all.

Nick

Forward from Corrie Jane:

Hello Daddy

Was I good this evening or was I *GOOD*? Sat in my boffin being frightfully Pedigree Dawg while you entertained the Nortons. Dreadful couple, Daddy. Too much ritz and glitz and bling-bling for my liking. Angelica Norton's sparkling diamond rings nearly blinded Nonnie and I hated the way Rexxie kept looking at his Rolex watch – stupid fellow went on and on to Grandee about it being the spoils of a successful business venture. Mrs P thinks they are a couple of rum-uns dressed up in designer labels, whatever that means. I heard her saying so when she and Emiline were placing the little fishy bites onto the serving dish ready to go through to the lounge. Emiline thinks Mrs P is rather quirky and was smiling as she went past me, leaving a little fishy bite in my boffin as she went. I love Emiline!!!

Eating the fish reminded me so much of my first day in the big wide world... I was sooooo frightened stepping out into the cold of an early London dawn. I sooo wanted to howl – but decided not to draw attention to my doggy self too soon. Where would I go? What would become of me now? I kept thinking of my Granpappy's advice, 'North is Home'. But which way was north? My poor doggy heart was beating fast as I trotted along the pavement. It was too late to turn back. The rubbish lorry had accelerated away and the service gate was closed once more. 'Goodbye, First Family. Goodbye,' I growled sadly, and was gone.

London is a wonderful city, Daddy, sniffs and smells everywhere. I soon forgot my fears and spent the first few hours of freedom acquainting myself with my new surroundings. It was a far cry from the Highlands, of course. No fragrant heather or rippling burns in the centre of Old Smoky – as London is fondly called – but lots of interest for a wee doggy on her Great Adventure.

There was plenty of grub, too, and I soon found a large piece of fish in a white wrapper in the alleyway beyond the apartment. It tasted doggy delicious, washed down with water seeping from an outside tap. I was feeling good. On and on I padded until I came to a street with pavements wider than the Coiltie River near my Highland home. All sorts of people were rushing along, some going to work, some out for the shopping and some just there for the sheer enjoyment of the day. Everywhere I looked there were shops stacked full of everything the humoan heart desires, and there were smart cafés, too – so a doggy would not starve. Then, I caught a glimpse of a really ragged mutt staring back at me from a big glass window. Dreadful creature! I barked at it, Daddy, and it had the temerity to bark back. It was in a dreadful state – and probably full of fleas – how dare it even look at the Lady Corrie-Rex Arabella Jayne o' Kerrowdown an' Drum in that angry way. I was furious and lurched at the window growling with all my might. People around me laughed, for it was not a real dog at all but my reflection in the window. I had become a raggle-taggle uncared-for scrap of matted yellow fur in my months with my First Family. How could they have done such a thing to me, the Chieftain's Grandaughter? Whatever would my Granpappy think? The shame of it all!!! I decided to head for home as quickly as I could. Granpappy would make me a posh doggy again, I just knew it. All I had to do was find him.

I raced along the street, but a dreadful thing happened. I found myself all tangled up in a net, scooped up and placed inside a wire cage at the back of a white van. The dog catcher had been called in by the security guards at the store with the big window and my day of freedom was at an end. How I wept...

That is all for now, Daddy, as my paws are hurting. This Personal Computer malarkey that my Granpappy recommends in 'The PDH' is all very well, but the little keys make my paws ache, I can tell you!

I am just popping into the kitchen to see if anyone thought to leave me a morsel for my midnight feast. If not, I shall be very cross, howl to be let out, and spend a good half hour chasing imaginary trails in the garden. I love the moonlight – don't you?

Corrie

From: Mrs Nonnie Kent@art studio.paint
To: NP Kent@home.uk

Hello darling. Did not want to wake you up after you spent such a long time trying to persuade Corrie to come in during the night. I blame the Norton's cat for sitting on the back fence pretending to be a statue. Do you think the poor pooch realises that dogs are supposed to bark at cats? Corrie spent a good half-an-hour transfixed, her head on one side, considering what to do. She is a very cute dog – and I do love her so – I just wish she had not kept you out in the cold for so long. I know you were very good about it all, insisting that she was Keeping Catto – but really!!!

Anyway! On to my exciting news!!! I have just had a telephone call from Rexxie and he really likes my sketches. I have been offered the contract to design the mural for *le Woodlands* – it's going to be the best eatery for miles around! This is the break I have been looking for!!! I can take some time off and do some drawings. Your idea of going to Scotland sounds wonderful. We could go at the end of the month at Masie's half term. Perhaps that little doggy was sent to us to bring us luck!

Love
Nonnie xxxx

From: NP Kent@home.uk
To: Corrie Jayne@dogmail.grrr

I hope you are thoroughly ashamed of yourself for keeping me up half the night. Stories are all very well and I really enjoyed reading about your adventures, BUT why did you spend all that time in the garden at 2am, if you please, just gazing at next door's cat? By the way he's just called Woo Woo not General Woo Woo. Let me tell you, Miss High and Mighty, that dogs bark at cats, cats arch their backs and spit a bit. Dogs then bark again and cats run off. It's a simple dog/cat thing. What were you doing just staring it out? I thought you had gone into a trance, refusing to move and looking all confused. Wise up and let's all get some peace.

On a lighter note, I really enjoyed the latest instalment of your adventure. I was so sorry to hear how your First Family treated you. Not all humoans are the same, thank goodness. I would love to hear more when your little paws are up to it. By the way, what exactly did your Granpappy say about emailing humoans?

Daddy

From: Corrie Jayne@dogmail.grrr
To: NP Kent@home.uk

My dear Daddy.

I am so proud that we are going to visit the Highlands of my Homeland. Nonnie is so clever, I know that she will paint a beautiful mural at the restaurant and what is more she has already told me that I can go with you all to the grand opening. Pawfect.

Just know this, General Woo Woo is the cat's correct name. He has been a battling cat all his life, that is why his ears are crimped at the edges and he has a few teeth missing. Goodness knows he has had a rrrrruff time of it with the Nortons. He was telling me all about it last night. We can talk by just staring. Beware, Daddy, Beware! They are not what they seem. I have a feeling they are related to the Wicked Dogrustlers o' McNabbit. I shall investigate and report back. Inspector Corrie to the Rescue!!! As for the entry in 'The Puppy Dog's Handbook' about PCs – it's a bit of a mystery really, but does tie in neatly with the next instalment of my story...

My first day of freedom was doomed to be my last. I had been picked up by the dog catcher and I was soon on my way to the *Home for Displaced Dogs* in central London. I could see the city from my cage at the back of the dog wagon as we trundled along the road. I was sooo upset, for lots of road signs were labelled The North. Would I ever get to see my Granpappy again? Worse was to come Daddy. The dog catcher was trying to be kind I know – but he read the bone shaped tag hanging round my neck and rang my First Family to come and take me back.

Winnie was in a furious mood when she arrived, I could tell. All practised charm to the warden – but she held me up and shook me, Daddy, when she got me to the car. She called me a Scruffy Flea Bag. Me. Little ME!!! How dare she! I squirmed and wriggled to try and get out of her grasp and 'The PDH' fell out of my back pocket. I growled and yelped and she released her grip for a moment and I fell to the ground, too. It did not matter that my hind leg was hurting, or that my tag had fallen off, too, so long as I was able to scoop Granpappy's book up from the dirt in the car park. I stuffed it back into my pocket before she saw it and made another dash for freedom. Limping badly on my poorly leg, I was soon far, far away from horrid Winnie and this time I hoped it would be forever.

Soon darkness fell on the big city. What a day it had been. I was now lost and lonely on the dark streets of London. It started to rain. We Westies hate the rain; it makes our fur curl up too much, a bit like Masie's hair when she comes out of the bath tub, all curls around her face. I remember I sat down in a shop doorway. The lights were very bright because there were televisions on inside. I decided to review the damage to myself. My hind leg was really sore. My fur was in even more of a state, caked in mud from the car park. I could hardly see because the rain was dripping down my furry face. Whatever would my Granpappy say!!! It is written in 'The Puppy Dog's Handbook' that a Westie's fur should be kept in immaculate condition at all times as befitting our high place in all of doggykind. I decided to read the passage to myself once more. But, when I took out the book it was in a worse state than I was, I suppose you could say that it was Dog Eared (hee hee). The section *PC is for...* was missing altogether. I felt vexed with myself, I can tell you. Now I would never know what the section contained. Then I happened to glance up – and there was the answer right in front of me. A large glowing sign in the shop window read:

So, there it was, my Granpappy wanted me to keep in touch through the Internet via Personal Computer. That was why he had written *PC is for...* in 'The PDH'. Trust him to be up-to-date with the very latest in technology. I was particularly impressed by the number of gigabytes – Westies love big meals.

So I am sure you will understand that when I saw your Amazing Dogaton Personal Computer standing on the desk in your office, I knew it would be the ideal way to try and find my Granpappy, and keep in touch with your good self, of course. Grandee promised that I would fall on my paws when I came to live in this house Daddy, and so far he has been right. Gone is the feeling of not belonging, gone are the hunger pains I felt that night, gone is the cold and damp of my fur on that rainy night.

It's a dog's life here, Daddy.

Night, night

LCJ

Subject: It's Showtime!

From: Lady Corrie Jayne@dogmail.grrr
To: NP Kent@home.uk

Dear Daddy

Do I look like the Lady Corrie-Rex Arabella Jayne today or do I not? How very kind of the Captain and Crew of the *Welfordia Bay* to send me a diamante dog collar. It makes me look so adorable. Masie teamed it up with a crown and a magic wand from her dressing up box and 'The Look' is complete. I cannot lift my nose any higher though – it just will not go – but I think I sooooo give the impression that I am a Pawfectly Posh Doggy. I might just let out a bark or two from now on – but please do not bank on it. Posh Dawgs just do not do that sort of thing. Hope you understand, dear boy. Well I would write more, Daddy, but I can hardly see the keys of the PC today – my nose being so high in the air. I shall have to practise more (hee heee). I have also changed my email address to Lady Corrie Jayne – please note!

Please say a big thank you to all my fans on the *Welfordia Bay* for such a fitting and delightful gift!

Lady Corrie-Rex Arabella Jayne o' Kerrowdown an' Drum, Countess of Wishing Well House, Millennium Drive. Very Posh Doggy – so do not ruffle my fur. Thank you.

 Reply from: NP Kent@home.uk

Hello MacMuck!

What do you mean giving yourself another email title and calling yourself a Countess– just because you have a new collar? You are still the same ragamuffin from the dog home – and today's escapades prove it. I have given up apologising for you. You are just a rascal – new collar or no new collar. It was all going so well. We hardly heard a woof out of you yesterday when the new collar in dayglow pink with diamante finish was popped around your scruffy neck by Masie. Nonnie thought a trip to the doggy beauty shop would be in order and I had to agree that you looked really beautiful when I brought you back from *Perfectly Pampered Pooches* yesterday afternoon. I thought you had turned over a new leaf – especially after reading your email from earlier in the day. But no. Whatever were you doing in Grandee's car in the first place? I think you had better explain.

Daddy

 Reply from: Lady Corrie Jayne@dogmail.grrr

Dear Daddy

Things happen to Westies, Daddy, and today was just one of those days. Grandee had left his car door wide open and I was just curious to see if he had any of those little mints left, the ones he keeps in the tray by the handbrake. They are my doggy favourite you know. I admit I got a bit carried away snuffling around in the front seat. How was I to know that the handbrake was not on properly and the car would roll down the driveway towards the orchard at the back of the house? It gave me such a fright. Dogs hate travelling backwards. Worse, they hate looking at people following a car travelling backwards shouting at a doggy to put on the brake. Dogs just cannot do that sort of thing, clever though we are. Grandee, Emiline, and Mrs P were all vying for front position. What a commotion. Then the car stopped all on its own, helped, of course, by the rockery. All in all though, things could have been a lot worse – apart from Mrs P falling over the bonnet of the car and Grandee crashing into her. Emiline thought it was funny and laughed and laughed. Don't be fooled by Grandee pretending to be angry. He and Mrs P spent the rest of the morning going through the racing pages looking for a horse's name that suited the situation. If I were you, Daddy, I would find out what they are backing at Hey Dog Bark today.

Lady Corrie-Rex Arabella Jayne etc wounded pride and no mints to be found; pawfectly awful!

From: NP Kent@home.uk
To: Nonnie@art studio.paint

Hello Nonnie. Have Grandee, Mrs P and Emiline paid you a visit this morning? If so, did they mention backing a horse this afternoon?
Nick

Reply from: Nonnie@art studio.paint

Yes. They were looking very smug because they had been to the Bookies already. This doggy stuff is getting too much, Nick. I am so afraid Grandee will lose the proverbial shirt before he's through. They are betting heavily this time and are thinking of going to the race meeting. They were talking of taking you and Corrie along. So be warned!!!!

As for me, I shall continue to slave over the hot paint brush. When are we going to Scotland? I need to have my drawings ready by the end of the month so that I can have my ideas on paper ready to get started when I get back.

Nonnie xxxx

Reply from: NP Kent@home.uk

Hello darling

Thank you for your email. You were right. The three of them are off to 'Hey Dog Bark' for the late afternoon meeting. I am going along to see that they do not get into any mischief – or bet too much money. Kiss Masie and tell her I will be back for bedtime stories. As for Scotland, we will discuss later.

Love you
Nick XXX

| From: | Grandee@greenhouse.is my office |
| To: | NP Kent@home.uk |

Hello Nick

Here are my top tips for the late racing today:

4.30pm	Peppermint
5pm	Rocky Rider
5.30pm	Dented Pride
6.15pm	Highland Fling

I picked the ones that closely matched that little doggy's latest escapades. I've rung Micky and Garge and they are meeting us at the Haydock at 2 o'clock. I thought I would take my car – and the wee doggy!!! I think it is so fitting that you have re-named the race course Hey Dog Bark – you have a wonderful sense of humour. See you later.

Grandee

| Reply from: | NP Kent@home.uk |

Hello Grandee

I am okay for 2pm. It will be good to see Micky & Garge. I think

I should take my car as I have arranged for Pete at the garage to collect yours and give me an estimate for the damage Corrie caused. Besides, Mrs P is wearing a large hat for the occasion. We may not get her, Emiline and Corrie in the back seat together with the hat!

Nick

From: Lady Corrie Jayne@dogmail.grrr
To: NP Kent@home.uk

Dear Daddy, I am too excited to sleep. Hey Dog Bark is a wonderful place – rich in trails to sniff, not to mention the goodies that came my way today. For the first time in a very long while I felt Doggy Adored. Micky and Garge really know how to spoil a lassie. A hamburger all to myself from their winnings. Grrrrrreat!!!

I was so glad that you decided to join in the fun at the last moment. Everyone was soooo disappointed when you said that none of the horses Grandee had picked would win. Then they all did. You said that if they won you would eat Mrs P's hat. That would have been a terrible thing to do. Even I could not manage to chew that. Mrs P is very fond of her hat – she bought it in 1962 for her wedding to Mr P. Good job for you that she was not offended. She did look pawfectly silly in it though. Dogs have never understood humoan fashion sense; but even I could see that a large pink straw hat with roses round the brim, did not match well with her best yellow and red striped dress and purple shoes. But when it started to rain it made a wonderful umbrella – and kept my fur from getting wet. Top Dog!!!

You know, Daddy, I really love Emiline. She brought along a doggy drooling picnic – and I got my own plateful. So fitting, she served my tucker on a silver dish after you told her I had re-named myself. She thinks I make a wonderful Countess. So do I.

Grandee is lovely too. I knew he had forgiven me for the Rockery Incident for when we picked him up in the car, he was wearing the MacDog tartan waistcoat. He held me on his lap all the way to Hey Dog so I could see out of the window. It was sooooo fitting for a Countess. How beautiful I looked today, Daddy. My dog collar sparkled in the sunshine as we sped along the motorway and it looked so good against my new short dog-hair style. *Perfectly Pampered Pooches* is top!!!

If I have one teeny regret – it's that sooooo many strangers came up to pat my head, quite flattening my hair-do. My fault, I think – they found me hard to resist as I pranced along, tail high in the air like a flag, my fur as white as snow on a winter's morn, and my collar sparkling like sunlight on the River Dee.

Countess Corrie

PS Now that we are in the money – when are you taking me home? I hope that I will be able to find my wee Highland Birthplace far away over the Mountains o' Doom. I hope that I can find my Granpappy. 'Remember: North is Home', he wrote. I was soooo proud you remembered this at the races when you backed Northern Starlight in the last race. That little horse romped home. Of course, I would have liked to do a jig just like Mrs P, Mickey, and Garge. I was soooo tempted to add a few woofs and barks of my own, too – but my new status as Countess forbids it, dear boy.

Well, must poddle off to my boffin. It's nearly light and I promised General Woo Woo that I would be waiting for him at the back fence right after I have barked at the Postie.

Lady Corrie-Rex Arabella Jayne o' Kerrowdown an' Drum. Picker of Winners at Hey Dog Bark. (And I certainly can bark! Although it's limited now that I am a Countess.)

 Reply from: NP Kent@home.uk

Hello Doglett!

You are still sound asleep and its past 10am. Never mind. Masie has invited General Woo Woo in for a saucer of milk and he is now stretched out in front of the Aga. I expect you will sort the situation out when you wake up. What did Granpappy think about Cats?   I'm sure he has written a whole section on the subject in 'The Puppy Dog's Handbook'.

Mrs P has only just turned up for work this morning – she overslept and is now busy making coffee. She has already counted her winnings a hundred times since she came in – the notes will disintegrate if she keeps this up. Hope she remembers to vac the carpets and polish the furniture. She seems a bit dizzy today. I think it's because she is still wearing her hat. I'm beginning to find the tuneless singing of the 'Bonnie, Bonnie Bank o' Loch Homeland' a bit much. Surely she means the 'Bonnie, Bonnie Banks of Loch Lomond'? Is the Loch anywhere near the Mountains o' Doom, little Countess Muck? Do tell – then you can fluff up your fur and we can drive to Scotland for our holiday tomorrow.

Daddy

THIS IS A COMPLAINT. Whatever were you thinking of by inviting next door's CAT in to eat my breakfast and then idly snooze away the morning in my very own boffin? I demand a new dvd immediately – and in the meantime I command you to **send that moggy home.**

Yours furiously
Countess Corrie-Rex Arabella Jayne o' Kerrowdown an' Drum – v put out so put the CAT OUT!

Reply from: NP Kent @ home.uk
Forward to: Nonnie @ art studio.paint

Okay Countess Huffy

I am almost convinced now that you really are writing the doggy emails. The only other person in the house this morning was Mrs P and she would not know how to switch on the computer – she has difficulty with the knob on the can of furniture polish. 'Pass that smelly squirty stuff,' she shouted from the hall this morning. All I did was ask if it was her day for polishing. 'Mr P never wanted 'is furniture smellin' o' lavender an' chamomile. You sea-folk are a right fussin' lot,' she grumbled.

I hastily assured her that I am not in the least fussy. Mrs P got quite upset. I then had to make her another cup of coffee 'on account of a terrible 'eadache'. (Too many beers with M & G yesterday.) She said she hadn't 'ad an 'oliday since Mr P passed away. Then she started to cry. (Dreadful stuff, beer, for making a person weepy.)

Don't know what Nonnie is going to say, Corrie. I felt so sorry for Mrs P that I have invited her to come to Scotland with us.

Daddy

From: Nonnie@art studio.paint
To: NP Kent@home.uk

I cannot be cross with you – even though it is supposed to be <u>OUR HOLIDAY</u>. Grandee was dropping broad hints last night about how beautiful the Scottish Highlands are in springtime. He will never forgive us if we take Mrs P to Scotland and not him and Emiline. So, hire us a four track and then they can all come. At least Masie will have plenty of people to tell her bedtime stories and keep her amused. You know I get cross if she messes up my paints.
See you later

Nonnie xxxx

PS There was really no need to make up the doggy email bit you know!!! I am still very worried about you – but not half as worried as I am about Grandee and the Hey Dog Bark stuff.

From: The Lady Corrie Jayne@dogmail.grrr
To: NP Kent@home.uk

Dear Daddy

What is happening regarding my new dvd? I need one urgently for my boffin. I cannot sleep in a dvd that Catty

has been snoozin' on. Hope he does not get any ideas that he can STAY HERE. He mutters about old campaigns he has fought while he is asleep and when he wakes, he gets up and finishes off my tucker and drinks my water. Thank goodness he does not like choccy biccies or a doggy could starve.

Thank you for your email. Good news that we are heading for my Highland Home. Mrs P should be pawfectly good fun. I am looking forward to sitting on her knee as we travel north.

Sorry, there is nothing about cats in 'The Puppy Dog's Handbook', so my Granpappy must have looked kindly on them, and of course, I will do the same. Now that I am a Countess I am very gracious. Although I am still doggy furious about the state of my boffin. Please note I have changed my email address again to THE Lady Corrie Jayne...

By the way, it was good of Rexxie Norton to invite you to play golf when he saw you this afternoon. He had been looking everywhere for General Woo Woo who has been away on a Campaign for three days – mostly in my dvd

(Grrrrr). Do tell Rexxie though, Daddy, that from now on a Countess cannot eat toffees. I think he meant well by offering me one – but it stuck fast to my back teeth. I thought it was super-glue in disguise.

Now where is my new dvd? If I don't get a new one, I shall have no alternative but to sleep on your bed tonight. (Hee heee.)

Countess

 Reply from: NP Kent@home.uk

Corrie!

Keep off our bed! You snore and you have doggy bad breath. What is all this dvd nonsense?   A dvd is the part of a computer that you use for playing films – but a DUVET is something we humoans sleep under when in bed. You are getting the advertisement for the Dogatron Computer all mixed up.

I have been into *Ye Olde Pet Shoppe* in Harborough today and bought you a dog mattress (MacDog Tartan, of course) and a matching lightweight doggy duvet for your holiday. It all cost a small fortune – I must be crazy!!!

Now please stop glaring at Rexxie Norton every time you see him, and the new duvet can be packed for our trip. Be nasty to Rexxie and General Woo Woo will get it instead.

Daddy

From:	Grandee@greenhouse.is my office
To:	NP Kent@home.uk

Nick! You are really spoiling that little Westie. But, I agree, she is worth every penny. She pulled out all the stops for us with the gee-gees on Wednesday so I don't blame you really. She loves the new mattress and doggy duvet in her boffin. She spent the whole afternoon guarding it against next door's cat. Scotland can be cold even in April so it's a good idea to take it with us, so that she does not take a chill.

It was good of Rexxie Norton to invite you to play golf with him on Saturday. Of course, I could make up a foursome with the Blonde Bombshell as my partner if you like. Then we can start our Scottish Adventure on Sunday. Dear Emiline has found us all a nice B & B just east of Gretna Green for our first stop.

Grandee

From:	Masie@playtime.is best
To:	NP Kent@home.uk

Deer Daddy

I'm practisin me emales agin. I am so xited abat Sotlan. D yoo reeely think Corrie wil find her home in the mowntains. Wil she want to stay there?

Masie

Dearest Masie

I am sure that your spelling and grammar are getting worse by
the day. I will help you with it over time. Do not worry your little
head, my darling – that little doggy loves this family too much
to want to stay in Scotland without us.

Night, night
Love Daddy

 From: The Lady Corrie Jayne@dogmail.grrr
To: NP Kent@home.uk

My Most Loyal Doggy Subject!

Thank you so much for my snugly new mattress and dvd –
sorry duvet. They are truly just what a doggy needs. I have
slept so well tonight – although I missed your big comfy bed,
too. As I am now a Countess, I shall not take offence about
your email. Just know that no-one is pawfect – except Nonnie.
You also snore and, worse – have smelly feet. But, I forgive
you. I also promise to stop giving Rexxie doggy-death-stares
– even if he is, as I suspect, a Wicked Dog Rustler o'
MacNabbit. Why else would he try to do me in with a toffee!!!

It was raining in the night, Daddy. And I was reminded… of
my cold night in London when, for the first time I slept in
the TV shop doorway. Sad to tell, it was not the only night
I spent on the cold streets of London. There were to be
many more while I looked for the way home.

At first it was fun, Daddy, foraging for food and sleeping rrruff where I could; keeping out of the way of the Dog Patrols and people who might do harm to the Chieftain's Lassie.

Soon it was summertime and the days were long and glorious – I found park benches and shady trees to rest under. There were titbits from the tourists and the laughter of happy children to help me through. But my hind leg was sooo painful, Daddy, my fur long and dirty and my tummy rumbled with hunger on more than one starry night. I was just a wee tramp of a dog. My pedigree had gone for ever. But, I vowed that one day, one fine day, I would find my way home. Remember: North is Home. I wandered and wandered, the seasons changed summer to autumn; winter to spring. I lost count of how many. Then winter came again. Suddenly, it was colder than I could bear – but with it also came A Breakthrough!

I was right in the heart of the city, the wind was blowing hard and all the leaves were falling from the trees. I was cold. It was a Sunday morning and in the distance I could hear the sound of church bells pealing. I thought about my Granpappy. Would he be looking out over the dark waters to the Mountains o' Doom, calling to his lassie? It was sooo cold that day and I longed for the log fires of my mountain home. I felt the shivers all along my spine and I knew that I would have the Last Calling before the winter was through, unless my fortunes changed. I decided to think about my situation over a little nap somewhere warm.

Keepin' to the walls along the street, I made my way, stiff and limping, though I was. I could smell food and it made my little doggy mouth water. There must be something good along the road ahead. I stopped and sniffed the air and then I spotted it – a big sign.

I was soooo excited I almost doggy-well collapsed. Soon I came upon a place where humoans come and go. A glorious place full of trails and sniffs and metal beasties called trains.

It was good. Dare a doggy explore? What harm would it do? I went up the escalator and down and along the shiny floors. Then a funny thing happened – it was Westie destiny. A loud voice from the gods boomed out: 'The next train to leave on platform nine is the seven-forty-five to Northampton'. How could a chieftain's grandaughter resist? North is Home! All aboard!!!

Another adventure was about to begin. I am now going out to howl in the garden for a while, Daddy. I hope you understand that even though I am now a Countess, I sometimes have memories of my Highland Home that make the longing to go back just too much to bear.

Corrie

| From: | NP Kent@home.uk |
| To: | The Lady Corrie Jayne@dogmail.grrr |

Dear Countess Courage

Thank you for the story. It brought a lump to this old sea-dog's throat. Glad you made it as far as Northampton and not a stone's throw away from your present loving home. You are still a long way from the Highlands, but we are off to explore them early on Sunday morning. Just as the birds start singing the dawn chorus, we will be away. I will pack your boffin and your dvd, sorry duvet, rest assured.

Meanwhile, no more howling either from you or next door's cat – the Nortons and Mani's daddy have all complained. Whatever is the matter with the pair of you?

Daddy

| From: | Nonnie@art studio.paint |
| To: | NP Kent@home.uk |

Nick, I have tried your mobile number and the house phone but no answer, so I expect that you and Grandee are concentrating on the golf. Thank goodness there is no money on this one!!!

Masie and I are taking Emiline and Mrs P into Northampton at 11 o'clock. Corrie is hiding under the stairs. I think she is telling me she does not want to come with us. We thought we would buy some woollens as it might be cold in Scotland next week.

Thought we would all have a Chinese meal from *Woks the Matter* tonight. Mani's daddy has a special offer on.

Love

Nonnie xxxx

Nick!

Great game – and we won!!! Rexxie might be a whizz in the city, my boy, but the golf course is still ours!!! However, if we follow his financial advice we could be rich v quick. We will mull it over next week in Scotland.

Whatever got into Corrie? She is a funny doggy. I think she had dug up your Lucky Green Sweater to wish you well. Pity it was so muddy and that she dragged it round and round Rexxie's legs before we could stop her. He was not very pleased. He likes to look smart at all times, part of his City Financier training. Then Corrie knocked over his golf bag and made off with his golf balls. That wee Westie is a handful at times, I admit!

She really growled at Angelica Norton when she tried to rescue the old sweater. Corrie shook it and showered her in mud for good measure. I thought she was going to bite the dear lady when she screamed at Corrie to stop. What is wrong with the rascally pup?

Spoke to Nonnie on the phone earlier. She has invited the Nortons to the Chinese meal tonight to make amends – also Emiline, Mrs P (who will no doubt be wearing that ridiculous hat) and me. Woks the Matter does a wicked chicken curry – I will pop into town and fetch it. See you at 7pm.

Grandee

Dear Daddy

I hope you have a very good reason for throwing your slippers at me when I was howling in the garden tonight. May I remind you that I am now Lady Corrie-Rex Arabella Jayne o' Kerrowdown an' Drum, Countess of Wishing Well House, Millennium Drive. I cannot let this situation develop without a comment. Westies have a reason for everything they do and I was howling to my friends at the *Poor Doggy Rescue Centre* some miles away for advice. So listen up, Daddy – here it is:

Be careful. Remember I was sent to this family for Special Reasons. I was v worried when I overheard the Nortons speaking to you and to Grandee tonight. Do not get mixed up in their money-making schemes. It will be dire if you do. I know that Rexxie has fine clothes and Angelica enough diamonds to outdo the stars – but I have been Keeping Doggo and I know that General Woo Woo is only fed on scraps. He is not a well-cared-for moggy at all and even though I do not want him snoozing in my very own boffin – even I do not begrudge him a saucer of milk now and then.

I cannot find *Norton* in 'The PDH' but while I was looking, the book opened at the page entitled 'The Wicked Dogrustlers o' MacNabbit'. My Granpappy had very definite views on them I can tell you. They are schemers, Daddy, people who mean you harm. They are very selfish, wanting the best of everything for themselves and don't care how they get it. Describes Angelica Norton pawfectly I would say. You do not need the pedigree name MacNabbit to be one Daddy. You are just born a MacNabbit. Now I am trying my very doggy best to show them up in their true colours – but they are very prrrrrrowfessional and it is very hard. But know this, Daddy, they are MacNabbits through and through.

The house is very quiet and still and a Westie cannot sleep for the worry of it all – but I will try my best to keep you from harm. I shall be Keeping Doggo all the time.

Night night, from The Lady Corrie-Rex Arabella Jayne o' Kerrowdown an' Drum, Countess of Wishing Well House, Millennium Drive. Very Posh Doggy – but keeping a silent night watch for you.

Subject: The Banks o' My Homeland

| From: | The Lady Corrie Jayne@dogmail.grrr |
| To: | NP Kent@home.uk |

Dear Daddy

I am writing this on your new lapdog so I hope that you get this email when you wake up tomorrow. Oh Daddy, it has been snowing in the Highlands! Westie's adore that kind of thing and look how well my diamante dog collar looks around my noble neck. It was so clever of your ship mates to send me one in luminous pink. It stopped me from getting lost in the snow. Not like Masie, Nonnie and Mrs P. They would never have been found if it had not been for Mrs P's pink hat. It had been a very long time since Mrs P had been 'snow surfing' as she calls it, and she certainly found lots of snow drifts to practise on. It has been very cold. Fortunately, those winter woollens that Nonnie bought last Saturday came in very handy. I bet you were cross with yourself that you left yours behind. Daddy, spring comes very late in the Highlands of Scotland. Just because it was warm and sunny when we left Millennium Drive, it does not follow that it will be the same two days later in the Granpappyion Mountains o' home. I am having a *wonderful* time.

Too-da-loooooo
The Lady Corrie-Rex Arabella Jayne o' Kerrowdown an' Drum Countess of Wishing Well House, Millennium Drive. Very Posh Doggy holidaying in the Highlands.

 Reply from: NP Kent@home.uk

Hello my little Westie! I found your letter. By the way my new computer is called a LAPTOP not a lapdog!!!

I have to admit, Corrie, this is turning out to be one of the best holidays I have ever spent. There is something for everyone here. I admit I had some reservations when I saw the snow yesterday morning – but here in the mountains of northern Scotland the weather changes as quickly as Nonnie's paint brushes.

You could have warned me to expect snow in the Highlands, you rascal! However, I managed to find lots of golfing sweaters and warm socks in the shops of Inverness – so things have turned out quite well. I especially like the one with the lucky white heather emblem on the front that Nonnie, Masie and you bought for me. (I did not know you received pocket money as well as Masie!) I am sure it has already brought me luck – I trounced Grandee at golf this afternoon – despite the cold and the fact that he cheats!

Dear Nonnie has done some beautiful sketches for the mural. I think they are some of her finest ever. The mountain air agrees with her, I must say she is 'sooo' beautiful!

Meanwhile, Emiline just loves the holiday cottage called Pettyvaich I found near Loch Ness. The old-fashioned kitchen range has been just what she always dreamed of. She is a wonderful cook – and we have all reaped the benefits of the dishes she has made for us. She is a treasure.

Masie has been *so* entertained. From the snow yesterday, to Nessie spotting with Grandee and me, she has been such a good girl and quite fancies herself as an artist just like her Mummy. It was good of Mrs P to buy her a paint-box – even though Masie got a bit carried away with the red paint. It was a pity she spotted you all over with red – but I am sure it will soon wash out.

Mrs P has made us all laugh. I have tried tactfully to suggest that she swaps the large pink hat for something more practical – but it falls on deaf ears. Now she is convinced that it stopped the family from being lost for ever, we shall not be able to part her from it. What ever possessed the three of them to walk to the top of the hill? I told them it was cold enough for snow. Off they all went, Masie in her track suit, Nonnie in her walking boots and Mrs P in the pink hat that 'wards off bad weather, this 'at does'. Then within an hour the weather changed and we all had to turn out and search for them. You are so good at sniffing trails – Sherpa Corrie to the rescue. Then you spotted the pink hat being waved by Mrs P and we soon had them all back to base camp.

I thought Mrs P was a bit over the top with the Hot Toddy – she has a liking for whisky and no mistake. Then there were her tuneless renditions of 'Scotland the Brave' that made you howl – but on the whole the holiday has gone well.

One sad part, I have not managed to find the Mountains o' Doom. Corrie, they are just not on the map. I expect it's your doggy name for the place where you were born, just like the Granpappyion Mountains! However, we have found plenty of Westies on our travels. You seemed so pleased to see them all. I hope they had good news o' Granpappy. I will be sorry to head for home tomorrow, but all good things come to an end.
Sleep tight.
Daddy

 Reply from: The Lady Corrie Jayne@dogmail.grrr

I hope that you know by the way I slept all the way home on your new lucky white heather golfing sweater that I had a pawfect holiday. Thank you for making this Pawfect Pedigree Doggy so happy with a wonderful holiday in my homeland. Oh Daddy! I am so loved and adored that my pedigree paperwork does not matter any more!

Yes, I managed to get a message to my Granpappy. He was soooo relieved to know that I have a good and loving home. I am sure you will be pleased to know that Granpappy has said that if I am a very good Westie I will able to retire in the Highlands. I shall have my very own CASTLE. This will be so fitting for my new title of The Lady Corrie-Rex Arabella

Jayne o' Kerrowdown an' Drum, Countess of Millennium Drive and so forth for about forty pages. Very Posh Doggy.

I think this family should doggy well move to the Highlands right away. It would be pawfect. I shall have carried out my promise to protect you against the MacNabbits and you can play golf all vacation long. Nonnie could paint her pictures and Masie would be fine at the village school in the glen. As for Grandee, there is racing at Thurso. We could find Emiline a castle with a big kitchen stove. Mrs P could live with us, too. So, when will you be taking me back to choose a Castle?

The Lady Corrie-Rex Arabella Jayne o' Kerrowdown an' Drum Countess of Millennium Drive, etc. Very Posh Doggy – and determined to go home sooner rather than later!

 Reply from: NP Kent@home.uk

Dear little Doggy

I wish I could make your dreams come true. But this is the real world – not a fairy story! Goodness only knows why I have just written that when I am emailing the family dog! We have had a good time in Scotland, I admit, it was a great success. Nonnie has her sketches all done and can start the mural – Grandee and I have decided to go with Rexxie Norton's new venture, and Masie has gone to school with presents for all her friends this morning. Mrs P is having a day off and I am going into Harborough with Emiline to buy an extra juicy bone for you. Before I go I will tackle the post. There is a whole stack of it and some of the letters look important. We are a popular family!

Daddy

Nick m' Boy

So sorry I was out when you called. I have just been into the bank to sort out my pennies. Then I came home and read your note. What a terrible shock!! I think you should tell Nonnie and Masie straight away about the letter from Tag and be Glad. No point in keeping this serious matter to yourself. I wonder why the Poor Doggy Rescue Centre did not pick up on the fact that at some time in the past Corrie had a microchip fitted in the scruff of her neck. Can you feel it? Now, her real family has been traced and want her back. I am heartbroken.

I know tagging is a good safeguard if you lose a pedigree dog. But, Corrie had been neglected for months and months. She is such a loyal little friend I can hardly believe she would just run away from a good and loving home. She was either snatched by dog-nappers or treated so badly that she just ran away. What a pity she cannot speak. Not that I do not believe that she emails you, of course! What has she said about her past?

Have you contacted the Mallory-Pickard-Watts family yet? I am concerned by the tone of their letter to you. Describing Corrie as an item of their property is just not on. She is a dog – not an old cardigan left on a park bench. What an attitude, threatening to report you to the police and take legal action to recover their possession. I am going to ring Tag and be Glad right away and complain. They should never have given out your address to the MPWs without contacting you first.

Grandee

What is going on? A juicy bone as promised, but a fairy cake from Emiline, a box of doggy chews from Nonnie, and a choccy biccie from Mrs P, who came to the house on her day off especially to give it to me.

Is it a doggy's birthday? I am doggy adored Bow Wow Wow!!!

Countess Corrie

From: Nonnie@art studio.paint

To: NP Kent@home.uk

Nick darling, we just cannot let Corrie go without a fight. I know how much you love her, making up all those funny emails about her to amuse us all. I am sure you can think up something from 'The

Puppy Dog's Handbook' that Granpappy advises when faced with such a dilemma.

You might as well know that I have been crying about Corrie all morning. The mural is not going well at all and everyone here at the restaurant is wondering what is wrong. I have decided to cut my working day short. My eyes are red and puffy and I look a right mess.

What are we going to tell Masie? She will be heartbroken to know that Corrie is to go back to the people who bought her in the first place. Well, all I can say is they should have looked after her better. She was in such a state – surely the *Poor Doggy Rescue Centre* will have something to say about it. Corrie must have walked all the way from London. It must have taken her such a long time; no wonder her paws were in such a state and her nails broken and bleeding.

I will be home at 12 o'clock – then we must discuss this matter and see what we can come up with.

Love you
Nonnie xxxx

From:	The Lady Corrie Jayne@dogmail.grrr
To:	NP Kent@home.uk

I demand to know what is going on! Whatever is the matter, Daddy? Why were you standing on the stairs shouting at us all to 'Stand by – stormy weather ahead'? Nonnie has been crying ever since she came home. Masie locked herself and me in her room until teatime – and had a tantrum AND it went unnoticed!!! Emiline cried all evening, and worse, Grandee kept blowing his nose and coughing like he has a terrible cold and I know he has not. As for Mrs P, she was dragging her feet and muttering darkly to herself. What was she doing here making all those pots of tea? No-one drank a single cup.

Is it me? What has a Westie done? Surely my suggestion of a castle in the Highlands, a Happy Holiday Home, could hardly cause such a reaction.

I wish to inform you that I am going to sulk in my boffin for a while and read the chapter in 'The PDH' entitled Humoan Behaviour. I shall see if my Granpappy can come up with a few answers.

The Lady Corrie-Rex Arabella Jayne o' Kerrowdown an' Drum, Countess of Millennium Drive.

Very Posh Doggy – and determined to go home sooner rather than later with or without a castle!

From: Masie@playtime.is best
To: The Lady Corrie Jayne@dogmail.grrr

Dear Coree

Is it tru y r going to live in Lundon. I thooourt u mite go an live in Sotlan but y lundon.

Masie xxxx

From: The Lady Corrie Jayne@dogmail.grrr
To: NP Kent@home.uk

Dear Daddy

I cannot reply to Masie – it's breaking the rules. What is all this about London? And why are you all creating such a fuss? Have you been promoted to the Admiralty?

If so, we can well afford a smart London home and a Scottish Castle. So good for those get-away-from-it-all weekends you humoans love to take.

Will I get a chauffeur?

The Lady Corrie-Rex Arabella Jayne o' Kerrowdown an' Drum, Countess of Millennium Drive.

Very Posh Admiralty Dawg to be.

Reply from: NP Kent@home.uk

Well, Doggy Adorable…

Sorry, but I have some bad news. I hardly know how to tell you – so I am writing it down for you to read. It seems that you were fitted with a microchip when you were a wee baby dog. It's a sort of electronic PDH. It's in the scruff of your neck. It has lots of information about you written on it so that if you are ever lost your family can find you again.

I took you to the Vet when you were ill and he must have scanned the microchip for his records. Somehow *Tag and be*

86

Glad were sent the information and they sent out a letter to your First Family to let them know where you are.

I was surprised that the Mallory-Pickards-Watts **do** exist, Corrie, it's not a story that someone has made up on an email as a joke for me after all. They want you back. They bought you and you are a very special pedigree West Highland White Terrier, with a string of pedigree names longer than both your back paws. I am impressed!

This family is heartbroken and we do not want to lose you. Sonsie wee lassie that you are, you have woven your way into our hearts. As I write this, I can see you in your boffin looking at Nonnie with your head on one side wondering whatever is the matter with us all. Believe me, I would gladly buy you a holiday home in Scotland – if only I could think up a way to keep you with us.

Love
Daddy xxx

 Reply from: The Lady Corrie Jayne@dogmail.grrr

Dear Daddy

Howling on a windswept day!!!

I will treasure your email forever. I have pasted it into the back of 'The PDH'. Daddy, you said that I am sonsie (meaning clever and beautiful) which I am, and that you LOVE ME!!! It's official – I am Doggy Adored. Best of all, you have said that you will buy me a HHHH Happy Holiday Home Hideaway. Daddy, there are over two hundred castles in Scotland and my Granpappy knows every one. Which one can I have? Glamis? Dunrobin? Urquhart? They all look just the doggy job!!!

By the way, this doggy is staying where she is ADORED. Wretched Vettie snitching on a poorly dog. How dare he!!! Next time I go in I shall give him a very rrrruff time, I can tell you.

Now that we have established that I am:

THE LADY CORRIE-REX ARABELLA JAYNE OF KERROWDOWN AN' DRUM, SIRE OF MARMADUKE OF MUNLOCHY LEADER IN WAITING. SIRE OF CHIEFTAN MACVIC, GREAT HOWLER O' THE MOUNTAINS AND LORD O' CULBOKIE, LORD OF THE GREAT GLEN, THE WISEST OF ALL THE WESTIES AND THE GREAT LEADER, & COUNTESS MAC RHONA OF THE WHITE FALLS O' LOCH BRAVE AND so on and so forth for at least forty pages, AND Countess of Wishing Well House...

I promise to be a good and sonsie doggy – that is until Sunday. Do not be sad, dear Daddy, I promise you that things will be so much different once we have established that I am STAYING HERE. Wishing Well House, Millennium Drive is my dear and loving home. It was what I dreamed of when I was a waif and stray. Granpappy has written in 'The PDH' that some things are worth fighting for – and my place here is just that something.

Here is a little more of my story...

I was a waif and stray when I stepped off the train in Northampton. I was in a doggy state I can tell you. Where were the mountains of my homeland? I could not see them and the air did not smell of heather and soft running mountain streams at all. Truth to tell, dear boy, I could hardly see – my furry fringe had long grown over my eyes and as for smell – I could hardly smell anything other than myself. I smelled bad!!! (Hee heee.) I had been on the loose for far too long.

I wandered along the streets sniffing for clues – then my fur ruffled in the wind just long enough for me to see a street sign:

THE MOUNTS

Oh joy, Daddy! The mountains of my homeland must be around here somewhere! I decided to shelter for a while against the wind. Perhaps my Granpappy would be able to find me? I gave a few little woofs so that he might hear me, and settled down to sleep in a doorway. How was I supposed to know it was The Mounts Police Station!!! Suddenly, I was lifted off the ground and into the arms of a burly Police Sarge called Jeff. He had just finished the morning shift and decided there and then to take me to the *Poor Doggy Rescue Centre* where his girlfriend worked.

I think I must have been doggy exhausted because I did not struggle to get away at all. Besides, he seemed nice – and he found a choccy for me in his pocket. It was my lucky day after all.

I must have fallen off to sleep again for things became hazy in my doggy brain from then on. It is just a blur of uniforms and disinfectant and being warm and soft voices bidding me to be a good dog. I was a worn out doggy and it could so easily have been the end of my story. But it was not to be, Daddy, I was destined to find a good and loving home – just like my Granpappy set down for me in 'The PDH'.

So excuse me now, I have work to do, a much-chewed bone to bury and General Woo Woo to consult. He is waiting for

me amongst the greenery of the rockery and he knows all about Campaigns. So let the battle begin!!!
Too-da-looooo

Corrie etc...

For the attention of Electro Engineer Nicholas P Kent@home.uk

From: Captain@Merchant Vessel Good Ship Welfordia Bay

This story of yours is set to run and run, Nick, and we have all enjoyed your emails. Don't give up on the Westie, try and pay the Watts family off. I am sure they will squeeze you for the last penny, but I know that you have only three more weeks left of your vacation and you can come back early on overtime, if it helps the finances.

I will telephone you this afternoon and you can let me know your decision.
Best regards

Captain

From: Nonnie@art studio.paint
To: NP Kent@home.uk

Nick

I have had a great idea and I have just rushed over from the restaurant to write this as the telephone at home is engaged! We could try and buy back Corrie from the Mallory-Pickard-Watts family. I thought I could have a sale of my paintings in the garden on Saturday morning. Emiline is here, and she and Mrs P have offered to rustle up some cakes in time for a Bring and Buy stall and Grandee is going to auction his services as a gardener to the highest bidder. There is time for us to advertise in the local paper. I am sure lots of people will come and support us. Pawfect as Corrie would say!

Nonnie xxxx

 Reply from: NP Kent@home.uk

Darling Nonnie

You work too hard already – but I think the sale of work is a wonderful idea. However, I've rung the *Welfordia Bay* and I am going back early (15th May) to earn extra money. I am joining in Houston so the flight out will not be too long.

So, whatever happens, we will have enough money to strike a deal for our pedigree poochette if her upper crust owners are willing to part with her. This family is really pulling together – Masie has even offered the contents of her piggy bank, bless her. That little doggy has stolen our hearts and put them in her back pocket along with 'The PDH'. She was sent to us for Special Reasons, Nonnie, I can see that now.

I will come down to the studio later and help you with the picture framing.

Hugs & kisses and full steam ahead!
Nick

From: Grandee@greenhouse.is my office

To: NP Kent@home.uk

Heard your news from Emiline – sorry you have to go back early – but that little doggy is worth fighting for and I am proud of you. I am really worried about Corrie. Will the Mallory-Pickard-Watts treat her well if they get her back? Did they neglect her when she was a puppy and is that is why she ran away? Maybe it will become clear on Sunday.

In the meantime, I will be busy gardening for the Corrie Fund. There are lots of people who cannot mow a lawn here, you know. I could make a fortune. Talking of which – do you have any tips for Hey Dog Bark? I am too upset to look at the racing papers today.

The forecast for Saturday is good, so tell Nonnie I will be around at 8am to set out the tables and chairs. Mrs P is making homemade ice-cream. I thought we could rig up some music and have quite a little garden party. I just hope we are not too gloomy!

Grandee

From: NP Kent@home.uk

To: The Lady Corrie Jayne@dogmail.grrr

Corrie – you promised to be good! It was a Bring & Buy stall – not a Try and Fly stall.

Who stole the cakes?	You did!
Who stole the salmon sandwiches?	You did!
Who caused chaos?	You did!
And who howled at the moon tonight?	You did!

What is going on?

Daddy

 Reply from: The Lady Corrie Jayne@dogmail.grrr

Here is a photo of me reviewing today's proceedings from a safe distance...

I know pawfectly well it is a Bring and Buy – after all I brought my very best bone along to help my Fund. So nice to see so many people in the garden, and all because of me. Even the local radio man came along to interview me. I am a star, you know. I looked sooooo beautiful today. I was adored by everyone. Besides, you cannot be angry with me – I might be gone tomorrow. (Hee heeeee.)

A doggy could not resist Mrs P's fairy cakes. They were yummy. But I did leave my very best bone instead! I know that she shouted 'We've been raided by that pesky dog!' when I took off with the salmon sandwiches – but I needed them for a Special Reason and I can doggy well assure you that you will not have to wait too long to find out why. (Heee heeee.)

As for causing chaos – I was DANCING. Everyone sat about looking miserable and so I thought I would cheer up the proceedings. So I made off with Mrs P's pink hat and chased all around the garden with it, dancing in time to the music. It did Mrs P so much good to get some exercise and me some good practice for my PLAN. Talk about rock and roll – you humoans know nothing! Of course, everyone laughed and the party began. The Bring and Buy was a hive of activity. Items brought and bought with such a haste it made me giddy.

Nonnie sold all her paintings and I heard her telling Grandee that she now has a stock shortage. Grandee's gardening services went to Mani's daddy, whose garden certainly needs it. All the cakes and sandwiches were wolfed down as the whole village and folk from far and wide turned out to help us. I was sooooo proud, that I let everyone hug me – although my new status as a Countess hardly allows such behaviour, I know. But we did make lots of money for my Fund.
Woof woofs!!!

Corrie

From: Masie@playtime.is best
To: NP Kent@home.uk

Deere Nonnie and Daddy

I had a luvly day – hope we can keep Cory. Pleze try.

Masie XXXX

Reply from: NP Kent@home.uk

Dearest Masie – we are all keeping our fingers crossed for Corrie – so sleep tight and let's hope we can offer enough money to buy your furry friend's future.
Night, night

Nonnie and Daddy XXXXX

From: NP Kent@home.uk
To: The Lady Corrie Jayne@dogmail.grrr

Hello Countess Corrie with the endless pedigree, and a happy knack of turning the most civilized discussions into mayhem. I have said it before... It was all going so well...

Hundreds of people who had heard of your plight, the press, AND the man from the radio station were waiting outside this afternoon for the arrival of Desmond and Winnie Mallory-Pickard-Watts and their two children Toby (age 13) and Fiona-Mia (age 15). I thought for a moment that their 4x4 off-road-monster-of-a-vehicle would demolish my gates, the speed they were going as they whooshed into the Drive. Out they got,

95

Winnie very red in the face and demanding her 'ickle wickle Babskins' be returned to them immediately as you had been 'losty-wosty' for three whole years. I am not surprised that you refused to look at her. I think I would have done the same given how they treated you AND being called by a soppy name like that.

In vain Nonnie tried to be nice by inviting your First Family in for tea. But they were having none of it. What a ghastly bunch! Desmond had a calculator out in a flash when he realized we had all been fund raising for you. Meanwhile, Winnie and Fiona-Mia were giving interviews for the Press, calling the reporters 'Daharling' and piling on the agony for anyone still tuned into the radio station.

I blame Toby for keeping his sunglasses on and I just wish he hadn't told Mrs P that he was trying to be a *cool cat*. 'We don't need any o' them, Master Toby,' she boomed. 'We got enough **cats** round 'ere as it is'. She waved her hat in the direction of both Winnie and Angelica Norton. What has she got against our dear neighbour?

Of course, I will never know if that was a signal for the real rumpus to begin – but begin it did. Whose idea was it for General Woo Woo to race through the gates carrying an enormous mouse in his jaws? You gave a little yap and the two of you took off right through the crowd. Winnie was in mid *Daharling*. She had just opened her large handbag for another handkerchief when General Woo Woo deposited the mouse in it then made a quick getaway by climbing right to the top of our willow tree. I never knew you could jump like that, Corrie. You snatched up the handbag and gave it such a vicious shake that, shouting at the top of her voice, Winnie just had to let it go. People were clapping. Dogs were barking from as far away as the Rescue Centre, and General Woo Woo was spitting like fury, as Mrs P waved her hat and yelled, 'That moggy 'as furkled us all'.

Mousey was able to escape with ease as you tipped everything out of Winnie's bag. She was hopping mad! 'Stop right there, you horrid red-spotted mutt,' she yelled, noticing Masie's accidental paint spats on your fur. Then she picked you up and shook you. 'Daft, deaf, and a Westie! How BAD CAN THINGS GET?' she hissed.

A terrible silence fell.

'Much worse for you, I hope. We will never, never give Corrie up now!' Nonnie positively growled, as she snatched you back, Miss Doggy Adored, and stomped indoors, slamming the front door behind her.

It took me ages to calm everyone down. Mrs P took a swipe at Winnie with her hat, then the crowd jostled the MPWs who beat a very hasty retreat back to their wagon, shouting at each other as they fled. I rapped on the side window for ages and at last Desmond opened it just enough for me to plead your case to stay with us. Despite boos from the crowd, a very hard bargain the MPWs struck, I can tell you. You have cost me a fortune!

I have now bought you, MacMuck, lock, stock and pedigree records. So, Nonnie and I are going to marvel over them as we enjoy a very large glass of wine. After the day we have had we deserve it.

Hope that you and Woo Woo enjoy your night in Masie's room!

Daddy

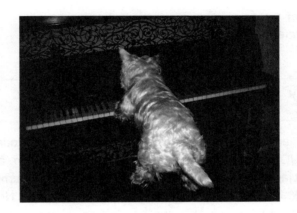

Subject: Trouble in *le Woodlands*

	From:	The Lady Corrie Jayne@dogmail.grrr
	To:	NP Kent@home.uk

Dear Daddy

I know that I am looking a bit rrruff today. I did far too much howling at the piano last night. I am soooo pleased that My Plan worked. It was so good of General Woo Woo to help me – he is the Master of Campaigns, you know. That is why I had to bribe him with the salmon sandwiches – but he certainly won the battle for us. It took him all week to find a mouse that big!!! And now that I am officially staying, and you have all mulled over my pedigree, we can settle down to the serious business of finding me **A CASTLE**.

Woof woofs
Corrie

 Reply from: NP Kent@home.uk

You are not the only one looking a bit 'rrruff' today (spelt ROUGH, incidentally), my dear doggy, I think we are all feeling a bit jaded after yesterday's events. Mrs P has not turned up for work this morning. Masie was late for school, and Nonnie will soon be back because she has left her sketch book behind. Poor old Grandee is gardening fit to bust at Mani's house and I am surveying the balance of my bank account. I have decided to donate your Corrie Fund to the *Poor Doggy Rescue Centre* and pay for you myself. I think the Doggy Centre rescued someone special in you and they should be rewarded for that.

Just one thing: thank you for sending all those downloads to me about the Castles of Scotland, even though they fouled up my in-box for hours! Drumlanrig is beautiful and the home of Brave Heart, and I agree Balmoral is in spectacular surroundings and Cawdor is just a gem – but none of them are FOR SALE. Corrie, it is not the done thing just to march up to the front door and announce that you are taking over. I would need to find somewhere that has a **FOR SALE** sign outside!

I also need to know how I would pay for it. I need a money-making-scheme to help things along and I promise you that a Highland Home Hideaway is yours! Any suggestions?

Daddy

Reply from: The Lady Corrie Jayne@dogmail.grrr

Dear Daddy

I did not quite understand how you humoans come by your boffins – Westie's just claim their territory you know – one fearsome round of growling and a little gnashing of teeth and the deal is done. This will be a bit more difficult, but you just leave it to me. I will do my doggy best to find something pawfect for us. I shall have the place to myself tonight while you are all out at the Nortons – then I can surf the net and haul in a juicy castle. (Hee Hee.)

Corrie

 From: Grandee@greenhouse.is my office
To: NP Kent@home.uk

All set for this evening? Hope this deal with the Nortons will make us all rich! I will meet you there at 8pm. In the meantime, I'm backing Jumping Jack Cat in the 4.30pm at Hey Dog Bark today. – it looks like a winner to me!!

Grandee

 From: The Lady Corrie Jayne@dogmail.grrr
To: NP Kent@home.uk

Dear Daddy

What was all the commotion when you came in last night? Emiline was not joking when she said you were all a bit tipsy.

How Grandee could drink champagne on a Monday evening is beyond me! Dreadful stuff – all those bubbles would get right up a doggy's nose and I am sure it tastes worse than stagnant water in a Highland pond!

Poor General Woo Woo almost had a heart attack when you knocked over the milk bottles at the door. He was just snoozing in the high branches of the willow tree pretending to be a panther (hee hee) when you all toddled along singing, dancing and acting v merry. Over went the bottles – startling the poor old pussy cat out of his wits. He took off out of the tree and was half way to Sibbertoft before he realised that he was not being shot at by a big game hunter. Poor old mogs that he is – his nerves are quite gone, Daddy. I am worried about him. I don't suppose the Nortons had any goodies left from their little do last evening? There was not a sign of a tasty morsel in my bowl and General Woo Woo has just scoffed my lunch. Typical!

The Lady Corrie-Rex Arabella Jayne o' Kerrowdown an' Drum, Countess of Millennium Drive. Very Posh and hoping for a Happy Holiday Highland Home as soon as possible!

From: Grandee@greenhouse.is my office
To: NP Kent@home.uk

Hello Nick

My head is a bit sore but I am still very excited about our new business venture with Rexxie and the Blonde Bombshell!!! There is always money in food, and buying a share in le Woodlands is sure to be a winner. I know we have had to take a mortgage out on both our houses – but the venture will soon make us enough profit to buy that castle you have promised Corrie. I think it is very good of the Nortons to let us in on the deal in the first place. The paperwork was a bit awesome – so many documents to sign – but I am confident we are doing the right thing.

By the way, I am off to Harborough to collect my winnings from yesterday. Jumping Jack Cat romped home at 20 to 1. I might be able to buy a restaurant all of my own the way things are going!!

Grandee

	From:	The Lady Corrie Jayne@dogmail.grrr
	To:	NP Kent@home.uk

Daddy, what have you done? I have been growling for weeks about the Nortons o' MacNabbit. Why didn't you listen to me? They are **BAD**, Daddy. I am so afraid we will lose our happy home I have decided to stay in my boffin all day AND PRETEND TO BE OFF MY FOOD.

The Lady Corrie-Rex Arabella Jayne o' Kerrowdown an' Drum, **Countess** of Millennium Drive. Very Posh Doggy and hoping to keep a Happy Home despite the MacNabbits.

Reply from: NP Kent@home.uk

I was wondering what has been the matter with you, sulking in your boffin with your back to me, refusing to eat, or even to go for a walkies. I thought Westies loved walkies. I was worried that you might be sickening for something terrible. I don't think I could take another Vettie bill at the moment.

Now I have read your email and all becomes clear! I cannot understand what you have against the Nortons. Rexxie is a perfectly respectable businessman and Angelica is kind and rather beautiful. They have been very good to Nonnie by offering her the chance to paint a spectacular mural in their new restaurant. It is going to be one of the best eating houses in the area. The chef is coming all the way from France to do the cooking. Monsieur Rennie is a world-renowned Cordon Bleu Chef and people will flock from miles around just to say they have tasted a dish he has made for them.

This is where Grandee and I come in. The refurbishment of *le Woodlands* is going to be very expensive, and Rexxie has decided to make owning it a partnership. Grandee and I have stumped up some cash and once the restaurant is up and running it will make a profit, Grandee and I can repay the loans we have taken out on our properties and eventually I will be able to buy you the Castle of your Dreams! Why am I explaining this to a DOG?

Daddy

 Reply from: The Lady Corrie Jayne@dogmail.grrr

Daddy, I know it is partly my fault for asking for a HHHH in Scotland – but the Nortons o' MacNabbit are bad people and will DO THIS FAMILY HARM.

Corrie

Reply from: NP Kent@home.uk

Here we go again. The Nortons do not mean us harm – but if you howl in the garden again for hours tonight, as you did last night, you are the most likely member of this family to have harm done to them!!!

Daddy

Reply from: The Lady Corrie Jayne@dogmail.grrr

You have been warned and my Granpappy clearly states in 'The PDH' that a baby dog can do no more. I must carry on with the business of the day. I have found us a castle in Scotland. It is a tad run down but it is barkgain, as you humoans would say.

Corrie

PS I wanted my dinner and a walkies really – but I had to make my point. Here is a picture of me taken by Nonnie on a previous walkies...

Licks and woofs

Corrie

From: Nonnie@art studio.paint
To: NP Kent@home.uk

Hello Nick

My masterpiece is just about finished. Is there any chance of you coming along to *le Woodlands* later and admiring my handiwork? I struggled to finish it before the tables and chairs arrived and I thought we could have a celebratory drink, just the two of us. It will be chaos here tomorrow because Rennie arrives in the morning to lay out his kitchen. Then on Friday it's the opening night...

Nonnie xxxx

From: The Lady Corrie Jayne@dogmail.grrr
To: NP Kent@home.uk

Dear Daddy

I must admit that Nonnie's mural looks wonderful. She has captured the spirit of a woodland so well. Best of all, she has painted me into the picture. She sketched me as I was looking out over Loch Ness towards the mountains near my Granpappy's home. Now I am part of *le Woodlands* too. Pawfect. I have dreamed about it all night – and now it is Saturday morning and no-one is up yet. It was so good of you to let me go to the opening night. So enjoyable, dear boy. Maybe was not so pawfect for you – but a Westie can surely be forgiven for getting a tad excited with such delicious tucker there just for the taking. (Hee heeee.)

The Lady Corrie-Rex Arabella Jayne o' Kerrowdown an' Drum, Countess of Millennium Drive. Very Posh and trying to act the real Top Drawer Dawg that I am supposed to be! (Hee heeeeee.)

 Reply from: NP Kent@home.uk

Hello you furry terror. I thought you might have turned over a new leaf now that we have established your pedigree. No such luck!!! I think you should give 'The PDH' a rest for a while – especially the chapter your Granpappy entitled Causing Chaos. You must know it off by heart. I knew from the first that it was a mistake to take you to *le Woodlands* for the opening night. But you looked so pitiful sprawled by the front door, looking at me with those big brown eyes, that I did not have the heart to deny you a trip in the caries.

I had hardly parked before I realised I was in for trouble. It was the way you made a dash for the restaurant and trotted right inside as if you owned the place personally. Rexxie was just gathering the VIP guests and the press together and you completely stole the show.

The plan had been to interview Rexxie and Angelica at their candlelit table enjoying a sumptuous first course served by Monsieur Rennie himself. Afterwards they were to be photographed next to the beautiful mural painted by our dear Nonnie. Before they knew what had happened, you jumped onto Angelica's chair and gobbled up all the lobster bisque before Monsieur Rennie could lift a ladle to stop you. Angelica tried in vain to lift you down, so for good measure you licked her face as well.

Monsieur Rennie was jumping up and down trying to swipe you with his chef's hat while Angelica screamed and shouted for me to DO SOMETHING! But what? Pawprints all over the tablecloth, and the press conference in ruins, what was I supposed to do? The Press loved it, of course, taking your photograph while you posed this way and that, woofing merrily at your painted face in the mural on the wall. Then, Rexxie assured everyone that your best trick was to 'play dead' but you were having none of it. I know he was joking, but did he really need to shake you so hard?

Then Mrs P arrived. I'm beginning to think that she is the one sending me the doggy emails. 'Good Evening, Revellers,' she boomed from the doorway. Everyone turned to stare for Mrs P was wearing an oversized fairy outfit, complete with gossamer wings and an enormous fairy wand. 'Welcome to The Woodlands where the fairytale magic is only surpassed by the fine wines an' grub dished up by Rennie the French bloke in the 'at,' she yelled, waving the wand in a most alarming fashion. 'This little place is the perfect fairy dell for evenings out. Just look how The Lady Corrie Jane o' Kerrowdown an' Drum is enjoying the fishy soup – it's just pawfect. That is why our dear Nonnie has painted her furry features into the mural on the wall. So, it just remains for me to release a bit more fairy dust and the merriment can begin!' With that she dowsed Angelica in glittery confetti and muttered a spell under her breath. I do hope for Angelica's sake that it was a good spell!

Suddenly there was laughter and cheering (and a few woofs from you) and the party began. What an evening! What a success!

Today's papers are full of praise for *le Woodlands* and the telephone at the restaurant has not stopped ringing all morning. It's booked solid for weeks. I know it is going to do well for us and I can return to sea happy in the knowledge that our investment will be a good one.

Daddy

 Reply from: The Lady Corrie Jayne@dogmail.grrr

Dear Daddy

I am having a horrid time of it today. The fishy soup did not sit well in my tummy – much too heavy for a girleen after all. I had nightdogs as I snoozed in my boffin today. It so reminded me of my time in the *Poor Doggy Rescue Centre*. Too much food gobbled up too quickly after months on the cold streets, played havoc with a little doggy's digestion.

I thought we would never get home. I was dog tired I can tell you. Even though I whined, Grandee could hardly tear Emiline away from the shiny restaurant kitchen filled with all sorts of pots and pans and new fangled tools, and best of all a very large cooker. Nonnie and you spent hours and hours talking to people and refilling their glasses, while Mrs P set to work filling up the dishwasher and waving her wand to 'magic' the dishes clean.

One thing I am sooo pleased about – there were a few goodies brought back for General Woo Woo. He loves to sneak into the kitchen and steal my dinner from right under my nose. I just hope the offerings from Monsieur Rennie sat more agreeably in his tummy than they would have in mine. It soooo saved me the trouble o' burying the lot in the garden next to my very best bone. I really did not have the energy for burying things today. One thing though – Woo Woo did tell me a piece of juicy gossip when I pinned him up against your golf clubs for a bit of fun. Drat! Must go – Mrs P is stomping up the stairs with the vacuum cleaner. She is still muttering spells under her breath! It would not do for her to find me here typing Daddy – so unwise of me to use the 'puter in the day.

Corrie

| From: | Grandee@greenhouse.is my office |
| To: | NP Kent@home.uk |

Success and Double Success, le Woodlands is a sure winner and Sugar Plum romped home at Hey Dog at 11 to 1. Picked it out of the paper this very morning. Mrs P reminded me of a Sugar Plum Fairy in her outfit last night, and the rest, as they say, is history! Mrs P and I both had a little flutter on the horse and now we are in the money once more! It was so fortunate that on Friday evenings she goes to her drama group held in the little hall opposite the restaurant. Last night was a dress rehearsal for the pantomime to be held later in the year. Mrs P had just noticed our car draw up from the dressing room window and she saw Corrie make a dash for it. She knew our greedy Westie would be looking for food and decided we might need some help. The woman's a genius. We should thank both her and our little doggy for making the opening go with such a bang. The fairy dust and the magic wand absolutely made it as far as I am concerned.

I was so proud. I thought that you and Nonnie made the perfect hosts – quite outshone Angelica and Rexxie. They

110

could have made more of an effort. Even though I am the first to admit that Corrie was a handful, Angelica made a terrible fuss over a few affectionate doggy licks. I suppose it was a bit annoying to be upstaged by next door's dog, but everyone thought it was such a good act and it certainly got our new venture off to a good start.

Grandee

From: Captain@MV.Welfordia Bay
To: NP Kent@home.uk

Are you all set, Nick? We dock in Houston tomorrow evening. See you on Monday. Ronnie the Shipping Agent will meet you at the airport and bring you out to the ship. Then it's up to Europe, back to America, over to the Far East, and then up to America and back to Europe, etc. The office is sending on your flight details.

Best regards
Captain

PS Chiefie Cookie wants to know if you have any good recipes from Monsieur Rennie.

From: Nonnie@art studio.paint
To: EE NP Kent@MV.Welfordia Bay

Hello Darling

I am missing you terribly. Hope you made it to the ship on time. Corrie was v naughty, hiding your socks while you were trying to pack. I note that she has a pair in her boffin for comfort. Hope they are clean ones! Now Masie has taken charge of your Lucky Heather Sweater and sleeps with it under her pillow. Otherwise, life here is boring without you – as usual!

We have had a statement from Nest Eggs Banking plc. We have a sizeable debt on our hands now that we have such a huge loan on our house to buy into Rexxie's business venture, and it frightens me a bit. I know that Corrie and Mrs P did a wonderful publicity job for us on opening night – it's the most popular restaurant in town. I am sure you will be pleased to know that *le Woodlands* is booked up solid for weeks. But, Rexxie has taken charge of the finances, so do not ask me how much money is going into the bank. We must be doing well though, and we should be out of debt soon.

Did Rexxie mention when we could expect a dividend from *le Woodlands* profits? I have re-read the contract and I cannot find anything definite. Also, I am a bit concerned that my account for the mural has not been settled yet. Sorry – it's late at night and I am worrying again... Miss you. See you in eleven weeks exactly!

Love

Nonnie xxxx

From: The Lady Corrie Jayne@dogmail.grrr
To: EE NP Kent@MV.Welfordia Bay

Woof woofs, Daddy

Rest assured I am going to Keep Doggo all the while you are away – and tell you about everything that is going on here. I am especially keen to keep tabs on the MacNabbits.

For a start, General Woo Woo is camping out in our back garden. It's part of his Summer Campaign, you know, and now my tucker is at risk all the time. I don't suppose he has anywhere else to go really, and he knows that he will be well fed at Wishing Well House. I was going to tell you the other day that the MacNabbits are away for a while, but Mrs P arrived to vacuum-clean upstairs and I am terrified she will mistake my tail for a ball of fluff and suck me up the pipe! Have you looked at the details of the castle I sniffed out for you? I want to go home!

The Countess. Very Posh Doggy in need of a castle.

From: EE NP Kent@MV.Welfordia Bay
To: Nonnie@art studio.paint

Nonnie!

Received your email. Everything okay here. Now loaded and setting sail for Europe. Darling, I am a bit concerned about the money situation myself. I did not realize that Rexxie had not paid you for the mural. We should also be getting a monthly dividend from *le Woodlands* starting this month. I don't know how much, but I do know that Grandee is really relying on it to pay his bills, so let me know if you do not receive the payments and I will contact Rexxie myself. In the meantime, please don't panic, I'm sure everything will be fine.

By the way, Corrie has sent me details of a castle in Scotland. It is near the Loch. It needs a lot of work to bring it back to former glory – but it has possibilities. Show the details to Grandee and see what he thinks. We still have a tiny pot of money left, so we could buy it!

Night, night
Nick xxxx

 Reply from: Nonnie@art studio.paint

Nick, Are you completely crazy? You surely don't expect me to believe that Corrie sent you details of a derelict castle in the wilds of Scotland? However, I gave Corrie a good ticking off about it all, just in case, and now she is sulking in her boffin and refuses to go for walkies with me. Help!!!

Nonnie

 From: The Lady Corrie Jayne@dogmail.grrr
To: EE NP Kent@MV.Welfordia Bay

Hello Daddy

I am still Keeping Doggo, although with Nonnie shouting at me over the castle and General Woo Woo stealing my tucker I have been a very upset doggy.

However, today I have Struck Back as per my Granpappy's advice in 'The PDH'. Grandee took me to see Vettie this morning because I have been a bit miserable. Pawfect. I waited until the dreaded injection then legged it right off the table, did a long wee all over Vettie's shoes then made a dash for the door. That will teach him to snitch on a doggy!!! Struck Back with a Vengeance!!!

Tee Hee Heeeeee – Corrie

PS Now hear this Daddy, the MacNabbits are up to something. General Woo Woo tells me that Angelica has her heart set on The Firefly Diamond. It is coming up for sale soon in a far off place across the sea. Check it out.

From:	Grandee@greenhouse.is my office
To:	EE NP Kent@MV.Welfordia Bay

Nick!

That little dog is a rascal and no mistake. Masie and I took her to the Vet's today as Masie was sure that Corrie was poorly again. She has been a bit quiet and no wonder with Nonnie shouting at her over the castle project. Corrie went into the surgery a little poorly dog. I was so worried. I had to carry her out of the car; she was so limp and whimpered when I lifted her up. A different story when I put her on the table! I swear I heard her laugh. Waited until the injection came out then WHAM! Fought like a haggis in heather, flew off the table yelping and barking, poor Vet got an eye full of antibiotics, then for good measure Corrie did a wee all over his shoes before making a dash for the door. The rascally pup must have planned it. Got him back for the MPW Fiasco!!!

She wagged her tail all the way home, gobbled up all her food and is now basking in the garden in the sunshine.

By the way – I put in a bid for the Castle Clouds and it has been accepted. Nonnie is not pleased with us – but she does not understand High Finance like we do.

Grandee

From: The Lady Corrie Jayne@dogmail.grrr
To: EE NP Kent@MV.Welfordia Bay

Dear Daddy

'Puter's hardly free these days. Nonnie is busy on it all the time, counting things up and doing complicated sums. She seems to be v worried. We had a visit from horrid men late yesterday evening. I growled and growled, but they were not in the least afraid of me. Nonnie cried and Grandee came round and he was v upset too and took the lapdog home with him. I am guarding my boffin against all comers and re-reading my Granpappy's advice on How to Growl to the Greatest Effect. Something's v wrong somewhere...

Corrie

From: Nonnie@art studio.paint
To: EE NP Kent@MV.Welfordia Bay

Nick, I still have not received payment for the mural and this has left a big hole in my finances. I am really worried because we have not received the monthly dividend Rexxie promised us from *le Woodlands* either. I tried to get in touch with him without success. I think the Nortons have gone away; the lights come on in their house each evening, but they could have installed a security switch.

Things are going from bad to worse at an alarming rate, I'm afraid. We had a visit from two men from a debt recovery agency late last night. There is definitely a problem with *le Woodlands* funding. I called Grandee round and he arranged a visit to their office this morning to find out HOW MUCH WE OWE and try and sort out what has gone wrong. I will call you on the ship's phone later.

Nonnie

From: The Lady Corrie Jayne@dogmail.grrr

To: EE NP Kent@MV.Welfordia Bay

Dear Daddy

I wish to inform you that I am now living in a VERY GLOOMY HOUSE in which THINGS HAVE GONE BADLY WRONG. I just know the MacNabbits have caused it!! What have they done? Nonnie is packing all the best china and Emiline and Grandee are taking down the beds. At a guess I would say the family is on the move. I hope I will be, too. I don't want to go back to the *Poor Doggy Rescue Centre*. I promise to be good just like my Granpappy advises in 'The PDH'.

Mrs P is going to pack the 'puter for Nonnie next. It will

never work again. I am going to join Masie on the front steps and we will keep each other company. What has gone wrong? Will whining help?

A Sad Doggy

	From:	EE NP Kent@MV.Welfordia Bay
	To:	Nonnie@art studio.paint

Here is a picture of a volcano we passed this morning on our way down the Med. It's called Stromboli. I am sending it to you as I think I can see more smoke coming out of my ears than out of the volcano. What in all that is seamanship is going on? Have we lost everything? Our home? Grandee's home? All our possessions? That weird dog with the endless pedigree? Is Masie okay? Are you still speaking to me?

I cannot get home as we have set sail for the Far East via America – but I promise I will get back as soon as I can and SORT THIS MESS OUT WITH MY BARE HANDS. Love you and Masie and Corrie – I bet her Granpappy has something to say about this in 'The PDH'. Please tell her to stop whining. Look after things as best you can until I get back to you…..

Nick

Subject: The Scrap Yard Dawg

From: Cool LCJ@dogmail.grrr
To: EE NP Kent@MV.Welfordia Bay

Greetinz, Money Mochine. Listen up. Didn't I tell ya the McNabbits would be pinchin' on me territory? Millennium Drive is a gonna an' now we is livin' at Number 1 Scrap Yard Row, the cottage juz down street from Mus P. But bow-wow Dads, big stylie snifsandsmellsandsuch and now Arnie (chief hound around these parts) 'as taught me to sooopeak in Scrap Yard Dawg, it's the bizzo, Dads! Times ain't sobad 'ere really. Thooough we are a bit CRAMPED an' Nonnie ain't fer chillin'. No way. Been a real Mean Momma for ages, Dads – shoutin' down the 'phone at folk and tryin' to make sense o' those sums you humoans are so fond of.

Emiline an' Grandee are cool – though Grandee's banned from gamblin' or any kinda fun at all really. He's diggin' fer victory in the back yard – sez we need veg for the winter chills as we are BROKE like.

Mus P she's in every day like before Dads an' now giving Nonnie 'an 'elpin' 'and at the studio. 'Okay Nonnie you poor lamb, let's mackle up some picture frames' she said the other day. Off they went on the bus. Changed everything back to almost normal, Dads, now Nonnie's doing 'er paintings again.

Meanwhile, me an' Masie are havin' a GREAT SUMMER. Built ourselves a den in the bushes behind the cottage. We've 'ad black feet for weeks and no one even noticed!!! (Tee hee hee.)

O' course things are heaps better now that Nonnie's electofied the lapdog errr laptop. Nowz I can keep in touch fer a while.

Great stuff!!! And keep smilin' an' bringin in the moolah I say.

When'z yo' back to the bothy, Dads?

Cool LCJ

PS Note me new email address – it's posher un me new bothy.

Who wrote this drivel? Isn't my life difficult enough without a DOG with a severe spelling problem? Whatever has happened to you? Snap out of it at once. The very idea! Referring to me as DADS – I demand an explanation.

How my dear Nonnie is coping is beyond me. I just wish I could get off this rusting bucket of a ship and return home and sort everything out. But, it will be weeks and weeks before that happens. We have so many different charters that we are getting giddy from changing course. Europe, America, Far East, it's like being on a merry-go-round.

Corrie, I still do not understand what has gone wrong. One minute we were riding on the crest of the waves of fortune, and the next, drowning in a black sea of debts. I was sure that *le Woodlands* restaurant was a sound investment. I had absolutely no idea that Rexxie and Angelica had run into trouble with it. Debts piled on debts that they hid from us. How could they?

Trust our dear Nonnie to sort it all out. She is a wonderful woman, Corrie, and I am proud by the way the entire family has pulled together while I am away. So, Nonnie sold our homes and told everyone we were down-sizing for a while. It's the *in thing* apparently – none of our friends suspects that we have lost ABSOLUTELY EVERYTHING AND WILL NEVER RECOVER.

I am pleased though that all the debts have been settled on *le Woodlands*. I'll have more than a few magic words to say when I get back, I can tell you. The air will be black with static when I get hold of the Nortons o' MacNabbit. I should have listened to you – after all, you were sent by your Granpappy to keep this family from harm. Just explain to me, please, how the MacNabbits have kept their house in Millennium Drive while WE HAVE LOST EVERYTHING – INCLUDING MY GOLF CLUBS AND BEST LUCKY WHITE HEATHER SWEATER. How could Mrs P take them to a car boot sale and sell them? Surely things are not that bad?

Yours from the bridge of the Good Ship *Welfordia Bay*.

Daddy

 Reply from: Cool LCJ@dogmail.grrr

Whoah! Chill yer boots, Dads. I've moved on with the furniture van see and adaptable to surroundin's. I can't be the Countess no more cos this cool doglett needs to blend in with the scenery. My Granpappy advises it in 'The PDH'.

It's all yer own doin', Dads – I told yer that Angelica was all trout and no pout – but you and Grandee were 'aving none of it. The outcome was always going to be in the MacNabbits' favour, my Granpappy sez so in the 'Andbook an' I quote:

'*Always note that few people can match the cunning of a MacNabbit!*'

They is BAD PEOPLE, Dads, **BAD!**

Meantime I have been checkin' out the howl on the street. Seems the MacNabbits have gone away for an extended 'oliday. Well, that's the Official Version, but the General Woo Woo whisper to me is they have gone to buy The Firefly Diamond, I was telling you of.

Angelica's CRAZY about gem stones – she was always eyeing up my diamante dog collar. I juz know they nicked off with all our money – took it out of *Woodlands* by the bag full leaving us to pick up the bills and them with enough dosh for The Firefly Diamond.

Simple innit?

Cool CLJ

 Reply from: EE NP Kent@MV.Welfordia Bay

Corrie!

I demand that you stop these terrible ungrammatical emails at once. I can hardly make sense of them.

Daddy

 Reply from: Cool LCJ@dogmail.grrr

Sorry, man. Me head's a shed these days so no can do re style of writin' emails. Juz remember that I'm blending in with the mixture 'ere Dads an' sooopeakin' in Scrap Yard Dawg. It would not do for me to be myself really – I'd just be given a goin' over by that HUGE black hairy monster over in the Scrap Yard. I'm playin' fings just like my Granpappy tells it in the 'Andbook.

'There will be times when it will be necessary to Fit In.

Although Bonny Westies must never forget our proud heritage, we must at all times be adaptable to any given situation. It is sometimes necessary to pretend to be a common dog and – if this is the case – be the most humble of all the common dawgs around. It will work every time'.

So that's wot I'm goin' to do whilst we're 'ere in the most run down part o' the village like. We are all keepin' a pretty low profile – 'ceptin' our Nonnie. Dads, she is still in a **fury** – turnin' out da pretty pict-u-ares like she's on a Paint Ball Weekend.

I blames Mus P. She bin givin' it large for dayz wid de pict-u-are framin'. I finks she's stock pilin' incase there is a shortage o' wood. Emiline's as bad, cookin', cookin' and cookin' on the ole fashioned range in the kitchen, Dads. Chief Cookie Rennie won't let 'er use the shiny pans in *Woodlands* – says 'e's keeping everything for his-self until he's bin paid. 'Orrid man! So every day its scones, and cakes, and meat pies made for sale – me an' Arnie ain't ever bin so well fed! Just wish ole Woo Woo wuz 'ere as well – but 'es gone orft on a Summer Campaign now that the MacNabbits left on their 'olidays. 'E knew 'e wouldn't get fed at all, Dads, now that we's left Millennium Drive.

Sundays are mad 'ere, Dads. Nonnie, an' Emiline, an' Mus P go off real early in Mus P's old van. Up wi' the birdies they are while Masie's still asleep an' Grandee's hoin' and mowin'. They do car boots and art shows an' craft shows all over the place. We really need the dosherola, Dads, and crossed paws it keeps comin' in.

Cool LCJ

Reply from: Electro Engineer Nicholas P
Kent@MerchantVessel.Welfordia Bay

Dear Cool LCJ

Please note my full title and email address – I am just trying to keep one thing in my life sane.

I understand it all now, thank you. I can hardly believe the MacNabbits deliberately stole everything we owned just to fund Angelica's love of diamonds. HOW DARE THEY. I am getting angrier by the minute.

Meantime, keep up the good work, Doggo!!!

Dads!!!

From: Mrs Nonnie Kent@scrapyardcottage.muck
To: EE NP Kent@MV.Welfordia Bay

Hi there Nick Darling

Long time away and too few emails. We are having a rough time here. We are in a terrible situation and I hardly know where to start – but a deep breath and here goes...

Everything has been sold, Nick, our home, Grandee's home, most of the furniture – everything. But from the figures I have put together, we will just about scrape through without declaring ourselves Officially Bankrupt. Better still – you will not need to stay on an extra month as we discussed when I rang the ship. Things will be a bit spartan – but I would rather have you back here so we can at least be a family again.

Our troubles stem from not reading the small print of the contract that Rexxie drew up for us to make us partners in *le Woodlands*. We should have taken legal advice first – but we were so sure the venture was a sound one we did not stop to think things through. Somehow we have been left with all the debts. Rexxie just took a huge commission for setting us up in the business. It did not involve him or Angelica at all – they were sort of agents for putting the finance together. He's not so much a City Whizz Kid but a Swizz Kid!!! The venture has proved very costly – with all the new furnishings and Monsieur Rennie's fees we did not really stand a chance.

However, by selling everything we have cleared up the debts and now that we have paid Rennie he has agreed to stay on for the next six months and help us turn things around.

I can hardly think past the fact that our home has gone, Nick. All our best memories were there. Worse, Grandee has lost everything too – even sentimental things that he bought for my Mum. He is in a terrible way about it all.

Mrs P has been so kind to us. She really is a national treasure. Thank goodness she was able to persuade Bert the Scrap Yard Man to sell this little cottage to us. It's in a terrible state – but at least we have a roof of sorts over our heads. It's a bit of a squash in here, but I am sure we will all manage until we can turn our finances around. Grandee has been mending and painting for weeks – and Emiline has managed to cook wonderful things on the old kitchen range. I've got quite a suntan from being outside at markets and car boot sales and Masie is having a good time in her garden den. We must count our blessings.

I'm worried, though. The Lady Corrie Jayne has barked and barked since we came here. She is permanently filthy, too – black paws and even blacker face and her fur is growing too long. I blame Arnie the Scrap Yard Dog. He is a big tough character and he is into barking, too! He has taken our little Westie under his wing – or would it be paw? He takes her for walkies across the fields most days – I think he has a soft spot for her!

School starts next week and I am worried about Masie, too. Suppose the other kids tease her about living in Scrap Yard Row? I know that lots of her friends have been here to play in the den and stayed for tea and Mani is here every day – so all I can do is cross my fingers and hope that things will work out for her.

I miss not being able to talk to you, Nick. I can't wait until you come home. The volcano picture made me smile – it's a much angrier mountain than the ones in Corrie's Homeland. We had such a happy holiday. I'm longing to go back one day...

You must understand, though, that I am still cross that you and Grandee bought a crumbling pile in Scotland. If only we had known what was to become of our home I would never agreed that you should buy a castle. Grandee says it's a tumbledown place – well, I know all about that from living here!!!

Well, I had better get back to work on the figures for *le Woodlands*. I am trying to discover where Rexxie banked the takings each evening when we first opened. They certainly did not go into the restaurant's account, that is for sure. Perhaps there is another bank account somewhere!

Phone me soon

Nonnie

 Reply from: EE NP Kent@MV.Welfordia Bay

Darling Nonnie

You are being so brave and you are doing a wonderful job of sorting things out. Not long now and I will be home. I think it will be sometime in October.

I wish I had not chosen to be a sailor. It's so difficult to be away while there is such a crisis. At least my salary is helping the finances along though, and I am relieved that I do not need to stay at sea after my contracted time to earn extra money. I would have to do a short trip on another ship – one with a problem – and that is always tiring. I am so proud that you are keeping our heads above seawater. I promise to make everything better when I get home. Whatever were the Nortons thinking of? Corrie was so right – they are the MacNabbits – not our friends. That is the hard part.

Nonnie, I know you are busy, but I need a bit of a favour. A diamond has come up for auction. It's a very rare one called The Firefly. Can you possibly find out where it was sold and how much for? It will have been in the papers I am sure.

Missing you – but only four more weeks to go. Please don't worry about the castle, it's a long term project to renovate it and we will all enjoy doing that when things have been sorted out at *le Woodlands*.

Love
Nick xxx

 From: Masie@scrapyardcottage.small
To: EE NP Kent@MV.Welfordia Bay

Hello Daddy

I miss you. When are you coming back to make everything better?

Love
Masie

 Reply from: EE NP Kent@MV.Welfordia Bay

Hello Masie

It's good to know that you have discovered Spell Check! When the leaves on the trees turn golden in the sunshine I will be coming home.

I Love You. Always remember that.
Daddy xxx

Things are looking up, Dads. Word is that you is on your way home. Cool. Arnie and me jus' waitin' to help you sort out the MacNabbits. Don't know when they will be back though, 'ouse 'as bin empty for weeks. Takes meself for walkies up to Millennium Drive these days – folks at 1 Scrap Yard too busy making ends meet to look after me. I don't mind so long as I don't end up back at the *Poor Doggy Rescue Centre* ag'in. Me an Arnie like to walk the walk an' talk the talk of an evening. Most folks *and dogs* scared o' Arnie 'ceptin me – but then ag'in I ain't forgotten me proud heritage yet!

Me an' Arnie are Keepin' Doggo like you said. Read off a chip paper juz lying in the street that The Firefly Diamond was sold for a record sum at an auction in 'Merica. It's the most fascinating diamond ever found. Sparkles like a firefly on a summer night. It was sold to an unnamed person... Now I'm not sayin' nuffin 'ere but there was a pix o' folks at the auction, Dads, an' one of 'em looks just like Rexxie MacNabbit. Me an' Arnie juz looking to rip 'is britches to pieces like when we find 'im – wever or not 'e's wearing 'em at the time. Arnie an me ain't decided yet.

Woo Woo will soon be back from 'is Summer Campaign now that the smoky bonfire season 'as started. That cat will know what 'as been 'appenin' an' then I will pass on the info' to ya. Gotta go. Nonnie juz getting' up. I can hear 'er paddin' round the bedroom. When can we go an' live in the Castle Clouds, Dads? I could wear me diamond dog collar and be posh ag'in. I miss bein' posh.

Cool LCJ

From: Grandeeinthegarden@no.weeds

To: EE NP Kent@MV.Welfordia Bay

Nick m' boy!

Here I am at last with a few words for you. I spend all my time gardening these days – I must mow nearly all the lawns in the village – as well as weeding the gardens. I spend a lot of time just thinking about things as I work. How did we ever come down to this? I can hardly believe between us we now own a tumble-down cottage at the back-end of the village. How I miss my own little place in Lime Tree Road All my best memories were there and now I have had to sell it. I am trying not to dwell on things at the moment, Nick, otherwise I probably would shed a few tears and that will never do. I'm just a silly old boy!

Nonnie has almost stopped being angry with everyone – but not quite. She has told me you are looking for some information on The Firefly Diamond. That's easy – there were lots of reports about it in the newspapers. Mined in one of the African diamond mines, it is set into a platinum pendant. Really good quality stones are set in platinum. As the wearer moves, Nick, it sparkles in every beautiful colour you can think of – like a firefly on a summer eve.

If you were thinking of buying it for Nonnie, lad, think again. It was sold in New York recently and made a fortune – buyer unknown but thought to be someone in the UK. Why do you ask?

I am really glad that you will soon be home again. It will be really good to see you. We can then try and sort out this mess we have made for ourselves. We are going to be a bit

133

cramped here at the cottage though, so Emiline and I thought we would head north for a few weeks. We could check on the Castle Clouds. I wonder what state it is in. If it is truly dreadful, I don't think I will tell Nonnie!!!

I thought we could take Corrie along. She has been a bit of a handful these past few weeks. She has a new friend – Arnie the Scrap Yard dog. He is a big, hard, mean character, I can tell you, and boy can he bark for Britain! Of course, our fearless little Westie barks just as well – if not better. It is mayhem when they get together in the evenings, woofing and howling for all they are worth, before they take off across the fields to the village. Mrs P has nick-named Corrie the Peskey Westie. I somehow don't think it is a compliment!!!

Let me know which day you intend to fly in and I will collect you from the airport. I can borrow Mrs P's old van – it's not very smart – but now I've fixed the engine it is reliable.

Grandee

From: Cool LCJ@dogmail.grrr
To: EE NP Kent@MV.Welfordia Bay

Wotcha Pops in de Harse!!! Good ta see ya back. Too bad ya came on stage without an announcement, Dads. Arnie an' me don't dig that sort o' thing on our territory see. We wos only chillin' in the lane when we saw you marchin' along wi' ya cases, see. Simple innit? We thought you wos Vettie come to give us some dreadful injection to make us quiet dogs. So we decided to do some Serious WGB (Woofin', Growlin' and

134

Barkin') to let 'im know it's our territory 'ere. We both 'ad a bit of a shock when you knew our names – didn't recognize you wi' the beard an' all. Too late by then, Dads. Arnie 'ad knocked you for six with one Giant Leap for Dogkind – 'es bin practisin' it for months and it was 'is Big Chance like. I 'ad done a big wee-wee all over your cases by then. They were new ones too. Sorry, Dads. No 'ard feelings?

Cool LCJ

 Reply from: NP Kent@scrapyardcottage.clean

Corrie!

I demand that you revert to Queen's English right away. Enough of this Scrap Yard dawg malarkey. You used to be such a well-mannered doggy. What happened to your new Countess status?

I warn you now that I shall have to bath you directly – you smell dreadful, nearly as bad as Arnie. In fact, I shall use the hosepipe Grandee has fixed up in the back yard and give you both a nice warm shower. 'Pawfect' as you would say. I am appalled at the way Arnie and you greeted me. He is a very bad influence on you. The way you both came chasing along the lane, howling and growling, was very frightening indeed. I realize that a guard-dog such as that big fellow has to do his bit to keep out unwanted visitors to the Yard – but knocking me completely off my feet is simply not on! I ache all over this morning and after such a long 'plane trip from China I could very well do without such treatment.

Whatever would have happened to me if Mrs P had not run out to rescue me? 'Stop fightin' yer master, yer pesky Westie, an' you, Arnie, you're just barmy. Pack it in', she yelled, running at you both with her yard broom. 'These two Yard Guards 'ave run wild all summer, Nick. I hope that now the autumn winds are blowin' you might persuade them to find a nice cosy fireside to dream by and leave decent folks to go about their business without being barked at!'

I couldn't have agreed more! So 'simple init' – shut up and scrub up and we will all get along just fine.

Daddy

From: Masie@scrapyardcottage.small
To: Nonnie@art studio.paint

Mummy, Mummy guess what? Daddy has come home. I was just looking at the golden leaves on the bushes of my den and there he was just standing at the gate. He's grown a beard, Mummy! He says he's come home to be a pirate and take back all our belongings. Hope he won't get into trouble with the policeman. Grandee and Daddy have just borrowed Mrs P's van and they are coming into town to fetch you home. Emiline is baking a cake — so hurry up Mummy — my Daddy has come Home!!!

Love
Masie xxxx

From:	Cool LCJ@dogmail.grrr
To:	NP Kent@scrapyardcottage.clean

Oh Pops! Wot 'ave ya done? Ruined me street cred as Second in Command in Scrap Yard Row that's wot. How could you? I juz gotta hark the bark man or I'm done for! This is big game territory round 'ere. I need a profile, see. How could you bath me in front of Arnie. It's not a Scrap Yard doggy thing ta do. Mind you, Arnie's in a worse state. Him never 'ad a shower before, Dads — wot with using Woof & Go to make 'is fur nice it's very nearly done 'is 'ead in. Poor ole Arn' — he ain't ever bin pampered until now — them fleas in 'is fur 'ad already died o' shock without the flea spray from Vettie. How are we gonna keep law an' order now, Dads? Now we smell like rose bushes on a summer breeze. It ain't a Real Dog smell at all. O' course its worse for Arnie now Masie's fixed 'im up with a tartan bow round 'is neck. 'E finks 'e looks like a Christmas parcel.

Goin' to sulk in me boffin for a bit an' think wot's best to do. I need an 'oliday.

LCJ

Reply from: NP Kent@scrapyardcottage.clean

Thank you for your email, Doglett. Now that we have established that I am indeed the Chief Hound around these parts we shall get along woof-erly as you might say. Both you and Arnie are looking much better for your wash in the garden yesterday. You do not have to be filthy to be a nasty person, I'm sure Granpappy has told you that in 'The PDH'. After all, the Macnabbits o' Millenium Drive were a really nasty pair of scavengers – and I never even noticed until it was too late.

Things are going to change around here, little family doggy. Until I can get my hands on Angelica and Rexxie, I shall spend my time working through the list of jobs dear Nonnie has left for me. I will start with mending the roof using lots of nails and even more hammering and banging. Then it's the turn of the wonky front door that creaks on its hinges when it is opened. I shall put on new front door with shiny red paint and a brass door-knocker, this very day. Next, I shall measure up for new windows, and then it will be time to take you and Arnie for walkies. I thought we might go as far as Millennium Drive. To walk the walk and talk the talk, etc…

Daddy

Reply from: Cool LCJ@dogmail.grrr

Night, night, Daddy, it's bin a really 'eavy day 'ere. Every time you 'ammered Arnie woofed an' Mus P shouted 'Shut up yer daft dog' from 'er upstairs window. You should 'ave waited until Mus P went off to town on the bus to 'elp Nonnie. Peace reigned as soon as that 'appened. Me an Arnie enjoyed the walkies, Daddy – and Arnie loved it cos you threw a ball for 'im to catch. Sez it keeps 'im *alert* like. He likes you, Dads, 'e really does.

General Woo Woo will be back any day now an' so will the MacNabbits. *The Spickerty Span Cleaning Co* were at their pad when Arnie an' me pranced by early this morning, Dads. If their croft is being cleaned up you can tell that they will be back shortly.

Meantime, I'm going on an 'oliday wi' Grandee an' Emiline. I saw a tent being packed into the back of Mus P's old van. Looks like it's going to be The Great Outdoors for a few weeks. 'Ope my HHHH is okay. Keeping me paws crossed – and then I can wear me collar an' everyfink will be all right, juz you see.

Corrie

From: Grandee@an internet café in thehighlands.scot
To: NP Kent@scrapyardcottage.clean

Well, here we are at the Castle Clouds tucked right way in the mountains, just like it said in the brochure. Emiline nearly had a fit when she saw it. Things are bad here, m' boy, and that is the understatement of the year. The whole place is a DERELICT RUIN – never been inhabited for years except by mice and worse. We slept in the van most of the night and are now trying to find a bed and breakfast place somewhere in the glen. I don't know how many more adventures I can take at the moment. Just tell

Nonnie that everything is fine here. I am attaching a beautiful picture for her!

Grandee.

This is the little river that runs just beyond the castle, Nonnie. It's very beautiful this morning and I am sure we will all love the Castle Clouds when it's brought back up to standard. If you look carefully, you can see the castle in the very, very, very far distance.

Love

Grandee xxxx

Subject: The Long, Long, Winding Road

	From:	The Lady Corrie Jayne@ an internet café in thehighlands.scot
	To:	NP Kent@scrapyardcottage.clean

My dear and loyal subject, Daddy. Here I am in the happy Highlands of my Homeland – where the mists gently kiss the mountain tops and Hurricanes Hardly ever Happen on a Monday. Unless it is one named Grandee. He is positively a powerhouse this fine day, my dear. We have been chopping back undergrowth and pulling up nettles and weeds. Emiline has built a HUGE bonfire and we are going to grrrill sausages and brew tea later on. Pretty much pawfect I would say. Although it is true that dear Emiline is not cut out for a great outdoor adventure such as the Castle Clouds Project, at least she has stopped crying. I must admit that she was hugely successful at keeping a little doggy warm and snuggled in her sleeping bag last night. It rained all night long, Daddy, and Emiline and I were very scared in case we got attacked by haggis. There is no running water at the castle – unless we include the water running down the walls inside. Last night we camped in the Great Hall – but it was open to the night sky. (Brrrrr.) Emiline said she thought the whole place was the PITS and insisted we slept the rest of the night in the van.

But today the sun is shining, and now we are in Inverness at a café where there is a 'puter. I thought I would just dash off a few lines to you while everyone else is occupied telling Grandee and Emiline stories about the Castle Clouds. There are hot mugs of tea everywhere on the table, Daddy, and scones just oozing with butter.

I am sure those canny Invernessian estate agents were right to sell the castle as a little Des. Res. With DEFINITE POTENTIAL. I admit, it did look a bit scary looming out of the mist last night, all dark and mysterious. There were gardens once – but the brambles and weeds took over long ago. There are stone steps to the stout oak door – years old! I have spent all day regally prancing up and down them – just suits my Countess status pawfectly. I have been dreaming of my retirement to my Happy Highland Holiday Homeland. Of course, I miss you all dreadfully at 1 Scrap Yard Row, and I look forward to more jolly times with Arnie and my old friend Woo Woo. Is he home yet?

I am going for a long howl over the Loch this evening – to

see if I can contact Granpappy. He will no-doubt have lots of sound advice on how to deal with the MacNabbits.

Woofs & licks
Corrie

 Reply from: NP Kent@scrapyardcottage.clean

Hello Countess MacDog!

How nice to receive a properly worded email from you after all this time. I am so glad you approve of our castle. I know it is little more than a ruin, but it is the perfect buy to give us all something different to think about.

I think Arnie is missing you – he waited patiently at the back door for you to come outside all day yesterday. He was so miserable he could hardly pluck up enough energy to take a walk with me. He seems much more his old self today though. He has barked all morning, chasing over the Scrap Yard after something or other. I had better go and investigate – he's just raced past the kitchen window. Whatever is wrong? Wait a moment – General Woo Woo is sitting on his back hanging onto Arnie by that nice tartan bow Masie gave him. Poor Arnie – I had better go and rescue him. Corrie, does this mean the MacNabbits are back too?

Daddy

From:	Grandee@an internet café in thehighlands.scot
To:	NP Kent@scrapyardcottage.clean

Nick! Nonnie! We have discovered something!!!! Emiline bought the *Scottish Highland Gossip* today – it's the local version of *Hello*. We were just thumbing through the posh person's party section at lunch time (exhausted after clearing a path to the front of the castle) and I tell you I very nearly choked on my clootie dumpling, for there smiling out at us were Rexxie and Angelica. They were guests of honour at an international money-makers get-together here in Scotland. They were both looking very glam I must say – and no wonder for Angelica was wearing her new purchase: THE FIREFLY DIAMOND. Corrie was right Nick!!! Angelica did buy it. But whose money did she use?

Grandee

From:	Cool LCJ@dogmail.grrr
To:	NP Kent@scrapyardcottage.clean

It's so good to go a travellin' but even better to be at home. No 1 Scrap Yard Row looked positively beautiful this evening as we drew up outside in Mrs P's old van. Grandee felt he just had to come back and show you the picture of the MacNabbits as soon as possible.

The sun was setting behind the Scrap Yard, lighting up the little latticed windows of the cottage, as we arrived. You have been very busy since we have been away, re-tiling the roof and putting in new windows. Grandee has made such a pretty garden and it was alive with the evensong of thrushes and blackbirds as I pottered along the path. A delicious smell of supper was wafting through from the kitchen.

A doggy loves an open fire, Daddy, so warming to the paws as the autumn mist steals over the meadows. My own comfy boffin was drawn up close to the hearth in the tiny parlour by Masie. I was soooo reminded of my first wee boffin at Granpappy's house. Pawfect. I snoozed and dreamed all evening until Arnie came to call.

What 'as got into that dog? 'E's in a terrible state, since 'is big fallin' out with General Woo Woo. Good job you were on 'and to patch 'im up, Dads – 'e could 'ave died out there in the Scrap Yard and no-one would 'ave found 'im underneath all that rubbish.

That cat Woo Woo got a bit carried away, see. He'd bin

145

sleepin' on the *Welcome* mat at our front door when Arnie spotted 'im. Arnie sez it's 'is duty to deal with foes. Trouble was – General Woo Woo felt the same an' 'e's got medals for dog fightin'. Poor ole Arnie didn't stand a chance really. Woo Woo bit 'is ears, scratched 'is nose, chased off round the Yard and then jumped on 'is back – said 'e made a wonderful 'orse for a pussy cat to ride on. Arnie was 'oppin' mad but could not get 'im off.   'Is pride and 'is street cred is in tatters. 'Ow will 'e cope? Good job you waded in and saved the day and the doggy for he had serious wounds too. 'E was good for you at Vettie's though Dads – better than I've ever bin.

An' now he an' Woo Woo 'ave eaten their supper in our kitchen eyeing each other up from opposite bowls – things are getting much better. Arnie, he don't get on w'cats; sez 'e read that somewhere in a guard dogs 'andbook that dogs an' cats don't mix. Woo Woo is not helpin' things; he thinks Arnie smells too nice to be a proper guard dog. I talked 'em both round though, an' I'm sure fings will work out. We are goin' to unite for now to sort out the problem wi' the MacNabbits Dads – sort of setting our own feelin's aside until we've got our property back, like. My Granpappy sez as much in 'The PDH'.

> **'Leave the humoans to shout and lose their tempers as much as they like – it's the doggy's job to get back everything belonging to the family'.**

See ya tomorrow, Dads – how's you fixed for a walkies wi' the three of us an' Masie?

LCJ

Hello Doggy o' mine. Yes, a walkies will be nice. How are you today? Do try not to slip into Scrap Yard Dog slang too easily. I have difficulty grabbin'onyermeaninglike. (Hee hee.) We were a bit cramped in here last night – but it was a very nice evening. Masie, Woo Woo, Arnie and you all trying to find the best part of the hearth to sit by while the 'groanups' sat around staring at the photograph of Angelica wearing The Firefly Diamond. Nonnie was really furious. She had already completed her sums and it looks as though Rexxie and Angelica stole from us and we did not realize they were doing it. It was all I could do to stop Nonnie from going to Millennium Drive to confront them. She has found false invoices for things that had not even been purchased, accounts unpaid, no takings being paid into the bank. No wonder we lost everything – and according to Nonnie, it all neatly adds up to the amount Angelica paid for The Firefly Diamond. But we need to prove it – so I urgently need a word with the MacNabbits before Nonnie gets to them first!

What is your Plan?

Daddy

From: Captain and Crew@MV.Welfordia Bay
To: EE NP Kent@scrapyardcottage.clean

Yes! Tell us the Plan and we will come and help you.

The LCJ Fan Club

From: Cool LCJ@ dogmail.grrr

To: NP Kent@ scrapyardcottage.clean

My Friends, Fans, Family, Feline Comrade, and Brave Dog of Canine Cunning – lend me an ear!!! Or a juicy bone!!! (Sorry Shakespeare hee hee.) I have learned that the dreaded MacNabbits are back.   We must watch their every move...

LCJ and the Dog Pack (everyone mentioned above).

From: NP Kent@scrapyardcottage.clean

U R G E N T   To everyone in the Dog Pack

I can hardly type I am so angry. It was my intention to deal with the MacNabbits MYSELF. So, this very afternoon I marched right up to their door, Arnie at my heels. Bang, Bang, BANG, I knocked and knocked. Angelica opened the door just a crack 'Shoo, Shoo you dreadful tramp of a man. Go away! You will get no handouts here – this is a nice neighbourhood – so be off with you before I call for help!' she shrieked, and then slammed the door in my face before I could utter a word!

I suppose I should take heart from the fact that she did not recognize me. It must be my beard, but TRAMP come on now. I admit I was wearing my painting trousers and Arnie does look a bit the worse for wear. But – TRAMP! I will never recover from THE INSULT.

Nick

Daddy, do listen. I tried to warn you about Angelica. I just knew how she would react when she saw you. The word from General Woo Woo is that she laughed out loud at her own cunning when she slammed the door on you. She knew it was you, Daddy; the whole village knows that you have grown a beard while you have been away. Please wait while I get the Plan together. The nights are drawing in fast – and under the cover of darkness we will all stand together as one and fight the MacNabbits on their own territory.

Corrie

From: The Captain and Crew@MV.Welfordia Bay

To: NP Kent@scrapyardcottage.clean

Hello Nick. Hello the Lady Corrie Jayne o' Kerrowdown an' Drum. We have a Plan too. The *Welfordia Bay* is sailing up to France. We could man a lifeboat, hop across the Channel to London and pick up the canal system all the way to the village. Pawfect!!!

Captain and Crew; or should I say the Seaboard Dog Pack!!!???

Reply from: NP Kent@scrapyardcottage.clean

Thanks shipmates – but then what would happen? I have not had an email from LCJ in days, Woo Woo has disappeared and Arnie's time has been taken up by old Bert at the Scrap Yard.

They have had a delivery of cars for crushing – noise and dust everywhere. Emiline has taken to her bed because of it and Grandee is camping out at the allotment he has just taken charge of in Sibbertoft. This family is falling apart.

Nick

| From: | Masie@schoolroom.learn |
| To: | NP Kent@scrapyardcottage.clean |

Dear Mummy and Daddy

I am writing this a t school because we are practising our typing skills on computer today. Did you know that there is to be an Autumn Barbeque in Millennium Drive? Everyone at school is going – and I would like to go too. M y friends say that we are too broke to buy a ticket. That's not true, is it? We all need a ticket because the Barbeque is being held in aid of the Poor Doggy Rescue Centre, and Angelica and Rexxie are holding it in their garden. Pretty please, may we go?

Masie

Reply from: NP Kent@scrapyardcottage.clean
To: Masie@scrapyardcottage.small

Dear Masie

I am sending this to your home email address. Of course we can all go to the Barbeque. We need at least 20 tickets because I have just rung the *Welfordia Bay* and a good many of the crew would like the chance of a good nosh-up in Rexxie's and

Angelica's beautiful garden. I expect Angelica will be wearing something extra special. They are quite the party animals these days, doing goodly works for all doggy kind. I can hardly wait!!!!!

Love
Daddy xxxxx

From: NP Kent@ scrapyardcottage.clean
To: Nonnie@art studio.paint

Dear Nonnie

Please read the attached email from our Masie. We really need to go to Angelica and Rexxie's Barbeque. I would not mind betting that it is Angelica who has spread it around that we are broke. Can you write back to Masie on her school email address and reassure her that we are able to finance 20 tickets. Please don't faint!!! Some of my friends from the *Welfordia Bay* are coming over for the occasion.

Love

Nick xxx

Reply from: Nonnie@art studio .paint

Darling Nick, it's a lovely idea. Will there be a ticket for Mrs P, too? We can have a lovely evening at R & A's house – and it is such a good cause. Besides, if there are so many of our friends around they might be able to help us with a diversion. We could slip away for a few moments and take a look in Rexxie's study. I know he always keeps his door locked but the *le*

Woodlands file will be in there and it will show all the dirty deals he did against us. We will get in somehow.

Nonnie x

From: Cool LCJ@dogmail.grrr
To: NP Kent@scrapyardcottage.clean

It's such a good idea of Nonnie's. That was my Plan all along. I will help you with the diversion, my dears.

LCJ

Reply from: NP Kent@scrapyardcottage.clean

This is one occasion when the 'groanups' can sort things out for themselves, thank you. A doggy must stay behind and guard the house.

Daddy

Reply from: Cool LCJ@dogmail.grrr

Daddy, I insist that you allow me to Organize the Diversion... it's all part of my Plan and as a COUNTESS I shall pull rank and CREATE A DIVERSION ANYWAY. After all, the Barbeque is in aid of the *Poor Doggy Rescue Centre*. So what can be more natural than a Rescued Doggy paying the event a visit. Pawfect.

Countess LCJ

I just wish I had read your email before we left for the Barbeque. I thought you were in a huffy mood all day – sulking in your boffin and then hiding your dinner underneath the *Welcome* mat at the front door. As I look through old emails we have exchanged, there are many times when I have written: ***It had all started so well.*** But here we go again…

Along the dusty Scrap Yard Lane we walked in a large and happy crowd towards Millennium Drive. The Captain, my shipmates, and me, all in our uniforms. I had even shaved off my beard for the occasion. Neighbours and old friends were so pleased to see us all and as the wine flowed everyone soon forgot Angelica's gossip about us. The dance floor was crowded as people bopped to the band. True – there was not an awful lot of food for such a large party; but Angelica has always been downright stingy where hospitality is concerned.

Rexxie and Angelica were amazed to see us standing there in the garden – and I thought there was a bit of awkwardness between us all for a start. But Mrs P soon dispelled any ideas that we were there for an ulterior motive by loudly shouting, 'Cap'n, come an' grab yerself an 'amburger afore they is all gone. Great party, Angelica, although I can 'ardly see it for that rock glittering around yer neck!'

I think that people were too mesmerized by Angelica's beautiful diamond pendant to think about food anyway – after all it was The Firefly Diamond glittering there for all to see in a thousand different colours. I was quite mesmerized myself. Trust Mrs P to put things into perspective though, as she popped on her reading glasses and peered at it closer. 'Wonderful wot they put in Christmas

Crackers these days!' she marvelled. Angelica was icy. 'It's real,' she sniffed. 'It's The Firefly Diamond!' Mrs P was very taken aback, 'Lorks; you mus' be miw-lion-er-es,' she crowed. 'Good job you's matchin' pound for pound the monies raised here tonight!'

I know that Angelica was trying to deny that she and Rexxie had any intention of giving such a huge single donation, but Mrs P was encouraging the crowd to clap so loudly that her words were lost. Rexxie stomped off in the direction of his study to get his cheque book – he was very red in the face.

Nonnie knew it was her chance. But how could she stop him from locking the study door again?

Enter the entertainment for the evening! General Woo Woo skidded across the lawn at an alarming speed, howling at the top of his voice – followed by barmy Arnie and the pesky Westie! Such a commotion – so little time for the rest of us to prepare ourselves. Soon everyone was trying to catch the cat/stop the dogs/get out of the way/stand well back as the three of you created chaos. The band stopped playing and sausages burned on the barbeque as the mayhem continued. Pretty much pawfect, I would say. Nonnie and I ran into the house. 'Rexxie, there's a fight,' shouted Nonnie. Rexxie sped off waving his cheque-book, appealing for calm. And while I Kept Doggo, Nonnie crept into the study.

Rexxie is such a neat and tidy person it did not take Nonnie more than a moment to find the *le Woodlands* file showing all the dirty dealings Rexxie had done to finance The Firefly Diamond. I scooped it up and tucked it inside my uniform top – and then we walked smartly back to the garden. As you know, by this time General Woo Woo had managed to shinny up the old oak tree where a few moments earlier the band had been merrily playing beneath its autumn boughs. It all looked very different now, instruments and sheet music scattered around and a large hole in the base drum. Arnie had apparently decided in the heat of the chase, to take a shortcut through it rather than round it. People were whispering, in awe of his strength. Meanwhile, Rexxie had a struggling bundle of muddy fur held at arms length. 'You mannerless mongrel! What do you think you are playing at?' he raged at you, our dear little Westie. 'No wonder you ended up at the *Poor Doggy Rescue Centre*. No decent family would put up with you. That's why you've ended up in Scrap Yard Row with your equally common owners'.

Arnie, trailing a broken set of outdoor lights, did a double-take and padded smartly back to look Rexxie right in the eye. Oh no! I thought to myself, it's the Giant Leap for Dogkind taking shape again. 'No Arnie. Stop!' I shouted, and managed to grab him by the boatman's neckerchief presented to him by the Captain. I was shocked. What an obedient doggy – he sat right down at my feet.

A dreadful hush momentarily spread over the proceedings before Angelica positively exploded with rage. 'Get out of here! You dreadful bunch of low life! You have deliberately ruined our evening. Get out of here. Get out!!!' And she snatched you right out of Rexxie's arms intending to throw you to the ground. It was my good friend the Captain who jumped to your rescue, scooping you into his arms as you flew through the air. Then he turned to Angelica and gave a stiff little bow. 'Madam, I pity every poor homeless doggy in the Rescue Centre if they only have you to rely on for help,' he said.

Everyone turned to leave – but just as I drew level with the old oak tree, General Woo Woo, howling loudly, appeared to lose his grip on the branch and careered earthward landing with a loud *S P L O S H* in a large bowl of trifle. The MacNabbits were covered in sticky jelly and cream.

155

Pretty much pawfect I would say. No doubt Woo Woo felt much the same. I'm sure he winked at me! So goodnight, little friend, sleep well. I hope that you have not suffered too many bruises. I will take you to see Vettie tomorrow.
Love
Daddy

Reply from: Cool LCJ@dogmail.grrr

Goodnight, Daddy.

Please do not reward my Cunning Plan with a trip to see Vettie. He has hardly recovered from my last visit. I am quite well really – nothing that a large juicy bone will not cure!!! I thought my Plan worked pawfectly, although old Bert was cross with Arnie for causing such a fuss. I was soooo pleased that you convinced Bert that Arnie was a real hero. Its quite gone to his doggy head! I hope that Nonnie can unravel the MacNabbits' file. Then we need to put into action Part II of my Plan. More tomorrow...

LCJ

From: Nonnie@art studio.paint
To: NP Kent@scrapyardcottage.clean

Hello Nick

Hope you have recovered from Angelica's little party. I have read *le Woodlands* file very carefully. At last!!! We have details of what Rexxie should have paid into the bank. It's a fortune! I know that Rennie's reputation as a chef is gold plated – but he's earned us thousands in the short time he has been here. Rexxie did not bank a bean, kept every last penny for himself! And I want it back! I do not mind a court case – but it's going to take a very long time to sort this situation out and I feel we need to buy our lives back sooner rather than later. But how?

Nonnie xx

Reply from: NP Kent@scrapyardcottage.clean

I quite understand, my dear. What are we going to do about it? I'm just about to see my shipmates off – and then I will pop in to see you. Fancy lunch?

Nick xx

From: Cool LCJ@ dogmail.grrr
To: NP Kent@scrapyardcottage.clean

Hello Daddy

I have been looking through 'The PDH' for advice. My Granpappy is of the opinion that what is ours should be in our possession, like my juicy bone collection! Sooooo, we just need to acquire The Firefly Diamond for a while then bribe the MacNabbits to pay us back for it in those notes and coins you humoans are so fond of...

Simple, innit! Just leave it to me an' the moonlight. (Hee hee.)

LCJ

 Reply from: NP Kent@scrapyardcottage.clean

Thank you Corrie – but I don't think the MacNabbits will be leaving such an expensive piece of jewellery around. It's probably kept in a bank vault somewhere.

Sadly yours…

Daddy

A few days later. . .

Well, my dear Daddy, I must admit Part II of my Plan was just about as pawfect as a Westie could get it. Arnie & General Woo Woo and I 'ad it worked out ta the letter. Juicy Bones all round, I say.

I must admit it was a bit cold out there in the moonlight, but me an Arnie 'ad a job to do an' we Kept Doggo in Scrap Yard Lane for hours. We knew that the MacNabbits were going to 'ave a late night, see, and we waited and waited until their big car came into view over the bridge back into the village. Curtain Up. Lights and Action, as they say on TV!!!

General Woo Woo was already in place – we just 'ad to fetch you, Dads, and take you for a late night run across the fields and into Millennium Drive. A midnight walkies, past the MacNabbits' house. Nothing better on a Saturday – even if you were a bit out of puff as we chased along the darkened street.

The lights were on and we could see hot mugs of cocoa being swigged by the MacNabbits in their lounge. General Woo Woo sprang out in front of Arnie, spitting furiously like a cat demented. Arnie let out an enormous **GROWL** an' the chase was on. Round an' round the garden we went cat, dogs, an' humoan all in a circle. I know you tried to catch Arnie – but 'e was like an athlete giving it large for the cause.

Angelica 'ad dashed upstairs to get a better view of what all the commotion was about. 'Be gone, you dreadful animals leave my garden at once!' she screamed in rage. (Can't be good for her, you know.) General Woo Woo then dashed through 'is cat flap at the back of the 'ouse and rushed upstairs to spit and howl out of the window right next to his mistress. Lights came on all over the Drive. Pawfect. A doggy loves an audience.

Angelica now joined by Rexxie, leaned out of the window further and shouted some more. A hair brush sailed through the air and landed at my feet, I yapped and growled louder than Arnie while you appealed for calm. Next a pillow sailed down – Arnie loves pillows. He bit it and tossed it in the air 'til all the feathers cascaded out over the lawn.

Angelica was positively spitting with rage by then. In a moment of madness, she threw her last missiles: her very best shoes – the sparkly ones that go with The Firefly Diamond. Pawfect!!! Arnie and I picked up one each and ran away over the fields to Scrap Yard Row. After all, it was way past our beddy-byes time.

Sorry about the rest, Dads. I know that the MacNabbits 'ave bin up all night looking all over the Scrap Yard for them

161

shoes. I saw Angelica turn a wrecked car over with her bare hands. She is **one scary woman**. Old Bert told 'er to clear orft as the Scrap Yard is private property. But she was having none of it. She was sobbing by then, shouting for her shoes, stamping her bare feet, and yelling. By now the villagers had gathered in the Scrap Yard with their torches at the ready. Everyone was searching for the shoes. Rexxie was in a terrible rage shouting at everyone to: 'Find those wretched dogs so that I make myself a fur hat out of the pair of them'. Charmin'!

'You leave those poor doggies alone,' yelled Mrs P from her bedroom window, her hair bristling with v uncomfortable hair curlers. 'It's yer own fault for throwing them out of the window at the poor doggies in the first place'. Everyone agreed with her as her window slammed shut with an awesome **WHOOSH**.

Meanwhile, Arnie's gone to ground somewhere in the Yard, until all the fuss 'as died down, and I shall be in my boffin until further notice. But, I will just mention this. You see General Woo Woo told me that one of the shoes has a false heel and that is where Mrs MacNabbit has been keeping the precious Firefly Diamond. A doggy loves a chewy shoe on a Sunday morning. Pawfect for keeping a doggy's teeth nice and strong.

Daddy, I look so well... with The Firefly Diamond around my noble neck. It sooooo befits my noble status as Queenzie of all Westiekind. Masie thinks so too. I shall never forget the delighted hugs she gave me as she slipped it over my head. Of course, I shall defy anyone who tries to take it from me – especially if their name is Norton o' MacNabbit!

Dear Daddy, once the fuss has died down let us all run away

to our fairy castle in the Highlands, so that I can tell my Granpappy that I beat a MacNabbit fair and square.

Let the bark-ening begin...

Queenzie

| From: | Grandee inthegarden@no.weeds |
| To: | Nonnie @art studio.paint |

Hello Nonnie, Hello Nick, Hello Mrs P,

Hope you are all okay after such a broken night. I have two visitors here at 1 Scrap Yard – Angelica and Rexxie. Not to mention that terrible cat General Woo Woo and barmy Arnie. They are guarding Corrie with their lives. The MacNabbits are trying to part our dear little Westie from the sparkling Firefly Diamond fixed around her neck. But Arnie and General Woo Woo are having none of it. I have never heard such growling and gnashing of teeth – and that is just from Angelica. Please forget packing for the car boot sale you were going to this afternoon and come home immediately before things turn ugly.

That little doggy of ours is Saving This Family from Harm, just as I always predicted. It is the ideal opportunity to sort the MacNabbits out to our satisfaction! And get back all that is ours! Personally, I can hardly wait!!!

Hurry!!! Hurry!!!

Grandee

T
H
E

E
N
D
I
N
G

My dear, and most loyal, of all humoans. It is with much regret that I today announce that this will be my last email. Something BAD has happened. You remember that Arnie and I had a difference of opinion about General Woo Woo? Well, Arnie was rummaging through the rubbish in the Scrap Yard this morning and he found (of all things) a copy of 'The Puppy Dog's Handbook' written by Granpappy for one of my cousins. The three of us turned to the page PC – you remember the page that in my own dear copy had long ago been destroyed. Well Daddy, sad to say, that PC does not stand for Personal Computer at all – it stands for Pussy Cats. Arnie was quite right – a little Westie is supposed to guard against Pussy Cats at all times to stop 'em stealing one's tucker!!! Of course, both Arnie and I will make an exception in dear old Woo Woo's case. After all, he is a General and his campaigns are legendary.

Rest assured though, Daddy, that I will always have my loving family's best interests at heart. I shall continue to look out for MacNabbits – especially after my success against Angelica and Rexxie. I am so glad they are going to sell The Firefly Diamond and give us back all that we are owed. We can have a proper home again – or even retire to the Castle Clouds. Pawfect.

Your most loyal and loving doggy friend:

CORRIE-REX ARABELLA JAYNE O' KERROWDOWN AND DRUM, SIRE OF MARMADUKE OF MUNLOCHY & LADY BONNY HEATHER OF THE GREAT GLEN; SIRE CHIEFTAN MACVIC, GREAT HOWLER O' THE MOUNTAINS AND LORD O' CULBOKIE, LORD OF THE GREAT GLEN, THE WISEST OF ALL THE WESTIES AND THE GREAT LEADER. DEAR GRANNY, COUNTESS MAC RHONA O' THE WHITE FALLS O' LOCH BRAVE, DEAREST AND KINDEST OF ALL WESTIE-KIND. SHOPPERHOLIC WITH HER V OWN HUMOAN FAMILY AND LOVED AND ADMIRED BY EVERYONE. And so on and so forth for about sixty pages...

And ending with CORRIE-REX ARABELLA JAYNE –
DEFENDER OF THE KENT FAMILY AGAINST THE
WICKEDNESS O' THE MACNABBITS AND
UNDISPUTED **QUEEN** OF ALL WESTIEKIND...
PAWFECT!

 Reply from: NP Kent@scrapyardcottage.clean

Earth to Corrie.
Earth to Corrie.
Come in, please.

Daddy

 Reply from: NP Kent@scrapyardcottage.clean
To: The Lady Corrie Jayne@dogmail.grrr

Earth to Corrie.
Earth to Corrie.

Come in please, and re-write the rules in 'The PDH'! Talk in
Scrapyard Dawg! Drive me to distraction! But most of all, JUST
KEEP ON WRITING THOSE LETTERS TO DADDY!

Daddy

THE END...

OR

IS

IT?

(Hee Hee Tee Hee Hee – Pawfect!!!)